With love,

Sharon

2002

SIMPLY TOO DELICIOUS

Simply too Delicious

SHARON GLASS

Credits

PUBLISHED BY	ATV (PTY) LTD.
AUTHOR	SHARON GLASS
PHOTOGRAPHER	JANYON BOSHOFF - JANYON & CAMERA
FOOD STYLIST	CHRISTELLE WEBER
DESIGN AND LAYOUT	PATRICIA BRAUNE - NOTION
SCANNING/DTP	SCOTT AND JENNY WATERSON
PRODUCTION MANAGER	TONI VENTURINI
REPRODUCTION	HIRT & CARTER CAPE
PROPS	LOADS OF LIVING THE MUSEUM STORE GLASSBLOWING INDUSTRIES PICK 'N PAY HYPERMARKET GRAND AND GROTTY
PRINTER	CTP BOOK PRINTERS, CAPE TOWN

PRINTED IN 2002 BY CTP BOOK PRINTERS, CAPE TOWN
ISBN 0-620-29104-4

email:	sharon@sharonsrecipes.com sharon@sharonsrecipes.co.za
website:	www.sharonsrecipes.com www.sharonsrecipes.co.za

Introduction

This book is the result of your enjoyment of my recipes. It gives me such satisfaction to know just how much they are being used and enjoyed. A recipe book is worth every cent if the majority of recipes are used again and again. A tattered, well-worn book is a sign of a good book.

What would we do without food?

It is about enjoying life to the fullest, filling our bellies, making us laugh and bringing people together. I love sharing wonderful fresh ingredients, different cultures and cuisines. I enjoy inspiring you and fuelling your enthusiasm to love and enjoy food as I do.

Happy cooking and eating!

Acknowledgments

A dedicated team of professionals (with whom I had the pleasure of working on my first book) have given their all to produce (if possible) a finer, more elegant, more beautiful result - Janyon's magical photography, Christelle's perfect attention to detail in the styling, Patricia's unique and imaginative layout and design and the actual production would not be complete without the professionalism and precision of Toni.

But the stars of this book are my immediate family who inspire me to reach for the sky, particularly my husband Anthony, who has been the driving force behind my achievements and without whose support this book would not have been possible. And big kisses also to Teri, Ricci and Jake for always being in the kitchen.

My entire family and all my friends who fuel my passion for food, and without whose love, tasting, testing, criticism, eating and more eating, these recipes would not be here.

All of you, too, have made this possible, and thanks for allowing me to share my passion with you.

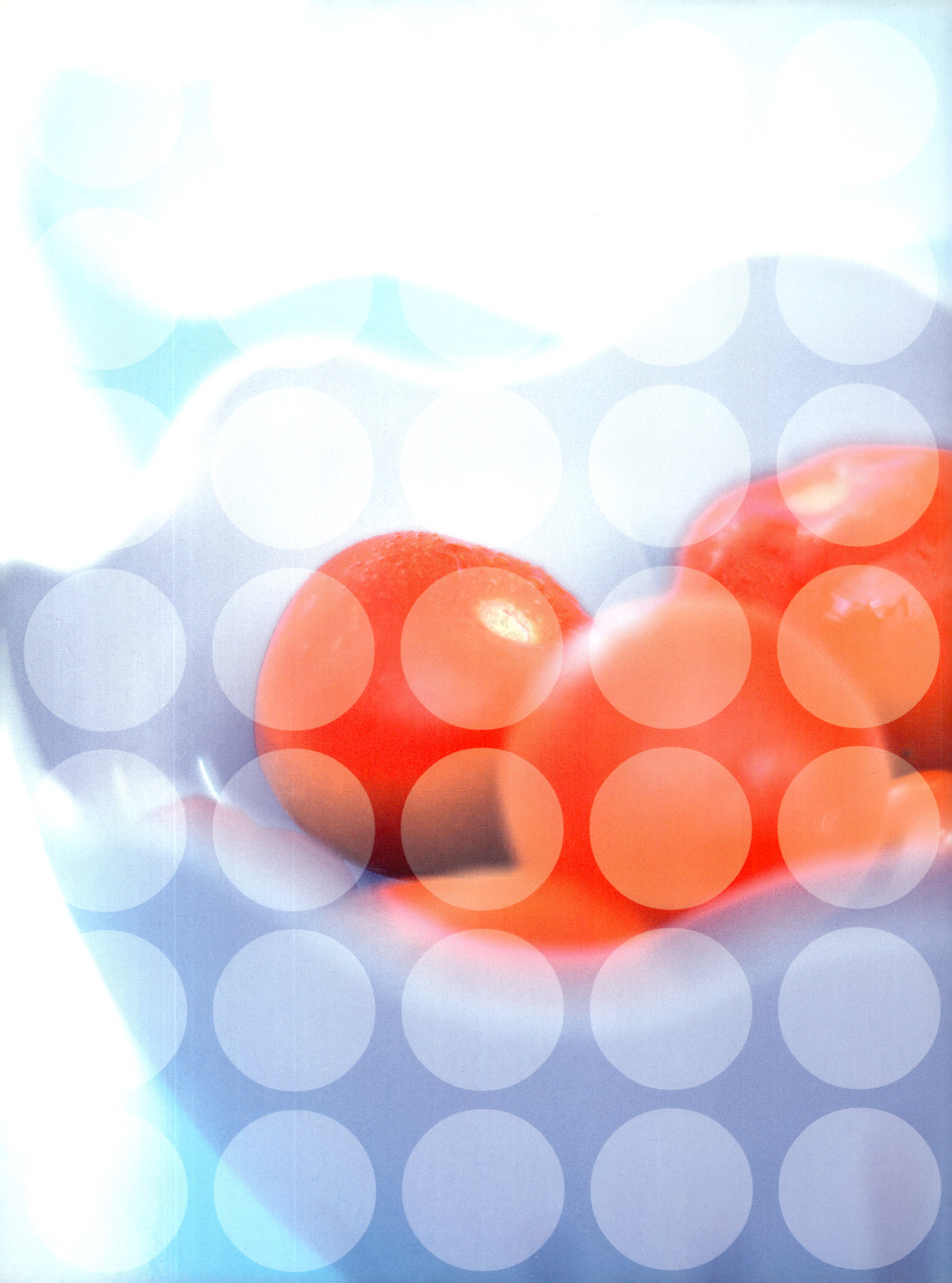

Contents

ROASTED TOMATO TARTS

Starters

ROASTED TOMATO TARTS

PHYLLO SPIRALS

MEXICAN CHEESE PIZZA

SMOKED FISH TERRINE

Starters

Start

We very rarely sit down to formal three-course meals. While desserts always remain separate, starters seem to have become a part of the main meal. They need to complement the main course, in that one should not fill up your guests so that they cannot fully appreciate the rest of the meal.

It therefore makes sense to use more vegetarian and fish starters to take the edge off rather than dull ones appetite. By the same token there is nothing wrong with only serving a stunning salad as a starter.

Once again my love for the versatility and ease of use of phyllo pastry continues.

QUICK AND EASY

- ROASTED ASPARAGUS WITH MUSTARD MAYONNAISE
- BRUSCHETTA AL POMODORO
- ROASTED RED PEPPER AND EGGPLANT DIP
- SWEET AND SPICY PEPITAS

RECIPES

- CHEESELESS GRILLED VEGETABLE PIZZA
- PHYLLO SPIRALS
- ROASTED TOMATO TARTS
- SMOKED SALMON ROSTI WITH WASABI MAYONNAISE
- TOMATO AND MOZZARELLA STACK WITH BASIL CREAM
- SMOKED FISH TERRINE
- MEXICAN CHEESE PIZZA
- PUMPKIN BREAD
- ASPARAGUS PHYLLO CRISPS
- BABY POTATO AND SMOKED SALMON SALAD
- MARINATED SWEET & SOUR SALMON FILLETS WITH HORSERADISH SAUCE
- ZUCCHINI MUFFINS
- SPIRAL BREAD
- MEZE PLATTER

ROASTED ASPARAGUS WITH MUSTARD MAYONNAISE

750g (1 1/2 lbs) FRESH GREEN ASPARAGUS
OLIVE OIL
HERBAMARE, SALT, PEPPER

Preheat grill.
Place asparagus on a baking tray lined with foil.
Drizzle with some olive oil. Season generously.
Place directly under the grill for 4-5 minutes, turning once while grilling. Cool.
Place on a platter until ready to serve.

DRESSING
125ml (1/2 cup) OLIVE OIL
30ml (2 Tbs) FRESH LEMON JUICE
30ml (2 Tbs) WHOLEGRAIN MUSTARD (PURCHASED or HOMEMADE)*
30ml (2 Tbs) CHOPPED PARSLEY
10ml (2 tsps) TOMATO CHILLI JAM*
30ml (2 Tbs) HELLMANN'S LIGHT MAYONNAISE

Process all ingredients in food processor until smooth. Can be spooned over centre of asparagus just before serving or served separately.

NOTE: Dressing can be made up to 3 days before. Keep refrigerated.

* See appendix

SERVES 6

BRUSCHETTA AL POMODORO

20 SLICES ITALIAN BREAD
OLIVE OIL FOR BRUSHING
2 GARLIC CLOVES, PEELED
COARSE SALT AND PEPPER

POMODORO
200g (7 oz) ROSA CHERRY TOMATOES, DICED
COARSE SALT, PEPPER
60-75ml (4-5 Tbs) OLIVE OIL
FRESH BASIL

Dice tomatoes. Cut basil with a scissors and add to tomatoes with olive oil. Season generously. Marinate for at least 1 hour. Place bread in 200°C (400°F) oven and toast lightly on each side. Sprinkle with a little salt and rub with some garlic if desired. Drizzle with a little olive oil, top generously with the pommodoro just before serving.

NOTE: Allow 2-3 per person. When buying Italian bread try and buy rolls or narrow long loaves.

SERVES 8-10

ROASTED RED PEPPER AND EGGPLANT DIP

1 LARGE EGGPLANT, CUT IN HALF LENGTHWISE
2 LARGE RED PEPPERS, CUT IN HALF LENGTHWISE
5ml (1 tsp) MINCED GARLIC or 1 GARLIC CLOVE CRUSHED
45ml (3 Tbs) OLIVE OIL
60ml (1/4 cup) PINE NUTS
5ml (1 tsp) GROUND CUMIN
2.5ml-5ml (1/2 - 1 tsp) CHILLI PASTE or CHILLI POWDER
45ml (3 Tbs) LEMON JUICE (BOTTLED or FRESH)
60ml (1/4 cup) CHOPPED PARSLEY
GENEROUS SALT AND PEPPER

Preheat oven to 240°C (440°F).
Brush skin of eggplant and peppers with olive oil.

Place vegetables on a baking tray lined with foil, cut side down. Cook until the eggplant softens, and pepper skins start to bubble - about 30 mins.

Allow to cool and then remove pulp of eggplant. Cut up peppers. Place both in food processor and process with remaining ingredients.
Season to taste.

Serve with lightly toasted pita, melba toast or Italian croutons.

NOTE: Keeps well in refrigerator for a few days. Serve at room temperature. Can be frozen.

MAKES 1 CUP

SWEET AND SPICY PEPITAS

1 UNBEATEN EGG WHITE
175ml (3/4 cup) SUGAR
45ml (3 Tbs) SESAME SEEDS*
1.5ml - 3ml (1/4 - 1/2 tsp) CAYENNE PEPPER
250ml (1 cup) PEPITAS (RAW PUMPKIN SEEDS)

Preheat oven to 140°C (300°F).
Coat pepitas in egg white.
Mix sugar, sesame seeds and cayenne pepper.
Pour pepitas into this mixture.
Place on sprayed baking paper on a baking tray.
Bake for 10-15 mins. moving occasionally until they change colour slightly and dry out. Allow to cool.

NOTE: This is an unusual snack to serve with drinks. Pepitas are very low in fat and keep very well in Tupperware for weeks.

* I like to toast my sesame seeds before using them, because it gives them a nutty flavour.

SERVES 4

ROASTED ASPARAGUS WITH MUSTARD MAYONNAISE

CHEESELESS GRILLED VEGETABLE PIZZA

You will love this pizza because it is so different, and without a tomato base and no cheese it becomes ultra crispy. It is gorgeous looking and tastes wonderful. Try it, you will make it again and again.

DOUGH
10g (1 Tbs) INSTANT DRY YEAST
500ml (2 cups) CAKE FLOUR
5ml (1 tsp) SALT
250ml (1 cup) WARM WATER
10ml (2 tsps) HONEY
30ml (2 Tbs) OLIVE OIL

DOUGH: Stir dry ingredients together. Mix moist ingredients together and stir into dry ingredients. Knead well until dough is smooth. Leave to rise in an oiled bowl until at least doubled in size and puffed. Roll out dough very thinly to fit into 2 pizza dishes or pans (30cm-12inches). Preheat oven to 200°C (400°F).

TOPPING
500ml (2 cups) EGGPLANT MAYONNAISE*
6 ZUCCHINI, SLICED LENGTHWISE
6 YELLOW PATTY PANS, SLICED
1 EGGPLANT, SLICED IN ROUNDS WITH THE SKIN
1 RED PEPPER, CUT INTO STRIPS
1 YELLOW PEPPER, CUT INTO STRIPS
125g (4 oz) PACKET SNOW PEAS
6 SMALL BABY CORN, CUT IN HALF
250g (8 oz) MEDIUM BROWN MUSHROOMS, WHOLE
1/2 RED ONION, CUT INTO THICK SLICES
FRESH ROCKET
FRESH BASIL
SEASONING

TO GRILL VEGETABLES: Place vegetables on flat baking trays lined with foil and season generously. Sprinkle with a little olive oil. Grill close to element until they are blackened. Turn whilst grilling. Set aside when all vegetables are grilled.

Spread the eggplant mayonnaise on pizza base, then grilled vegetables on top of mayonnaise in no particular pattern. Top with pieces of broken rocket and basil. Season again. Spray with olive oil spray.

Bake for 20-25 mins or until golden (crust as well). Makes 2 large or 3 small pizzas.

* Eggplant mayonnaise can often be purchased ready-made from a deli counter in your local supermarket. If not available, simply use the pulp of 1 cooked eggplant processed until smooth with 175ml (3/4 cup) mayonnaise.

SERVES 8-10

PHYLLO SPIRALS

An outstanding, make ahead snack with vibrant colours from the fillings and the crispy phyllo pastry. These are sure to appeal to any palate.

8 SHEETS PHYLLO PASTRY
UNSALTED BUTTER FOR BRUSHING

1) 150g (5 oz) SPINACH, SHREDDED FINELY AND SLIGHTLY WILTED
   200g (7 oz) FETA, CRUMBLED
   1 EGG YOLK

2) 250g (8 oz) WHITE MUSHROOMS, SLICED AND FRIED
   1 ONION, SLICED AND FRIED
   250ml (1 cup) GRATED MOZZARELLA or TUSSERS

3) 250ml (1 cup) CHEDDAR CHEESE, GRATED
   3 SPRING ONIONS, SLICED
   45ml (3 Tbs) SUN-DRIED TOMATOES, FINELY CHOPPED

OREGANO FOR SPRINKLING

Mix together each group of above ingredients in separate mixing bowls.

Brush 4 sheets phyllo with butter and place them on top of each other.

Spread 1/2 of each mixture in rows down the length of phyllo.

Roll up phyllo tightly from left to right in a long roll and brush outside of roll with butter. Repeat procedure for remaining half of mixtures.

Refrigerate rolls cut side down for at least 1 hour covered with plastic wrap. Remove from fridge and cut into 2cm (4/5 inch) slices before baking. Place cut side down on a baking tray lined with baking paper.

Bake 180°C (375°F) for 15 -20 mins.

NOTE: Phyllo spirals can be frozen unbaked, but must be cut into slices first. Defrost in the refrigerator overnight before baking. If not baking the rolls immediately, then place cut slices in the fridge well covered until ready to bake.

MAKES ± 28-30

CHEESELESS GRILLED VEGETABLE PIZZA

ROASTED TOMATO TARTS

A truly wonderful combination of colour, taste sensations and aroma, this gorgeous picture is worth making. A complex taste is created through the sweetness of the base combined with the saltiness of the tomatoes and the peppery rocket and aromatic basil.

1 x 200g (7 oz) ROLL PUFF PASTRY

10 ROMA TOMATOES, CUT IN HALF
45ml (3 Tbs) OLIVE OIL
SALT AND PEPPER

Preheat oven to 180°C (375°F).

Place cut tomatoes, cut side down in a roasting pan. Drizzle with the olive oil, sprinkle with salt and pepper. Roast for about 40 minutes uncovered. Pour off some of the juices. Continue baking for another 20 minutes. Remove from oven and cool slightly. Peel off any blackened tomato skin.

WHITE SUGAR FOR SPRINKLING
1 EGG, BEATEN FOR BRUSHING

Roll out puff pastry to fit a loose bottom tart tin (about 24cm-9 inch) (or 6 individual tart tins), allowing a thicker edge on the sides of the tin with the pastry. Prick base all over with a fork. Brush base and outer edges of pastry with a little beaten egg. Place tart tin on a baking tray.

Place in a preheated 200°C (400°F) oven for 18-20 minutes or until pastry is golden. Check during that time that the tart does not puff too much. Press gently with the palm of your hand if it puffs too much during the baking. Remove from oven. Sprinkle a little sugar on pastry base.

Remove pastry shell from the tin and place on baking paper on baking tray. Place pre-roasted tomatoes on the baked base, cut side down. Grated Mozzarella or Tussers can be sprinkled on the base first if you like a little cheese. Season tomatoes with salt and pepper. Reduce oven temperature to 180°C (375°F). Place tart in the oven again to bake for another 15 minutes or until golden.

Serve with a few sprigs of basil and some shredded rocket broken on top of tomatoes and sprinkle with salt.

OPTIONAL: Sprinkle a little grated parmesan on the outside crust of tart before baking with the tomatoes.

NOTE: Tart must not be served too hot, or the tomatoes lose their flavour. The base and the tomatoes can be made ahead of time, and combined to bake just before serving.

SERVES 8

SMOKED SALMON ROSTI WITH WASABI MAYONNAISE

This makes such an attractive starter and the combination of textures and tastes is spectacular. Be sure to make enough because your guests will gobble them up. They can be served with drinks or as a plated hors d'oeuvres with 3 rosti per person.

POTATO ROSTI
4 MEDIUM - LARGE BAKING POTATOES, COARSELY GRATED
½ ONION, FINELY GRATED
45ml (3 Tbs) FLOUR
SALT AND PEPPER

Mix all ingredients together. Squeeze out as much liquid from potato mixture as possible. Heat a little sunflower oil in a medium frying pan. Oil should not be more than 1 cm (½ inch) thick. When oil is quite hot, fry and only turn when browned. Drain on a paper towel.

500g (1 lb) SMOKED SALMON, CUT INTO STRIPS

2 AVOCADOES, CUT INTO THIN STRIPS

125ml (½ cup) HELLMANN'S LIGHT MAYONNAISE
10ml (2 tsp) WASABI POWDER*

TO SERVE: Place a drop of wasabi mayonnaise on the rosti, then a roll of smoked salmon and then strip of avocado. Grind some black pepper over just before serving.

NOTE: The potato rosti must be made the day you serve them because they won't remain crispy. Do not cover them or they will become soggy.

* See appendix

SERVES 8-10

SMOKED SALMON ROSTI WITH WASABI MAYONNAISE

TOMATO AND MOZZARELLA STACK WITH BASIL CREAM

As a stunning plated starter, or as a buffet platter this looks amazing and people will "ooh and aah" at your creation, which took only a few minutes. What better way to start a meal? Each stack is a portion, so allow about 3 slices of tomato and 3 slices of cheese per person.

18 SLICES TOMATO
18 SLICES MOZZARELLA

BASIL CREAM
30g (1 oz) PACKET FRESH BASIL
125ml (½ cup) SWEET MAYONNAISE
250ml (1 cup) FRESH CREAM
2.5ml (½ tsp) CHILLI PASTE or POWDER
SALT & PEPPER

Process basil and mayonnaise in the food processor. Add cream, chilli paste and seasoning. Do not over process or the cream will become butter. Make stacks of the tomato and mozzarella on a large platter or individual plates. Spoon the basil cream around the stack and decorate with a basil leaf. Sprinkle with lots of black pepper.

NOTE: This can be prepared and plated early in the day. The basil cream can be made up to 2 days in advance and kept refrigerated.

Avocado can also be added in between for extra colour.

SERVES 6

SMOKED FISH TERRINE

There is nothing like a fish starter that can be made ahead of time. This one is delicious, very simple, very colourful, very rich and can be adapted in many ways. It can be made in a large loaf tin or in individual ones. Serve this with one of the scrumptious breads in this section.

500g (2 cups) FULL CREAM FIRM SMOOTH CREAM CHEESE
80ml (⅓ cup) HELLMANN'S LIGHT MAYONNAISE
30ml (2 Tbs) RED HORSERADISH, DRAINED VERY DRY
15ml (1 Tbs) FRESHLY CUT CHIVES OR SPRING ONION
SALT & PEPPER

Mix all ingredients together.

500g (1 lb) SMOKED SNOEK, MACKEREL or PEPPERED MACKEREL - Remove excess bones and flake.
4 LARGE AVOCADOES, MASHED WELL*
30ml (2 Tbs) HELLMANN'S LIGHT MAYONNAISE
DASH OF PAPRIKA
45ml (3 Tbs) FRESH LEMON JUICE
SALT & PEPPER

Mix all ingredients together. Line a loaf tin (25cm-10inch) with plastic wrap. Spread ½ cream cheese mixture on bottom. Cover with ½ of smoked fish. Spread ½ avocado mixture on top. Repeat 1 more layer of each, ending with avocado. Cover top layer with plastic wrap. Press down gently with your hands. Refrigerate and allow to set for at least 3-4 hours, or overnight. To unmould: Remove top layer of plastic wrap. Place a serving platter on top of tin. Invert and remove other plastic wrap.

*Handy Tip: Immerse whole unpeeled avocado in a bowl of boiling water for 1 minute before cutting. This prevents blackening. Always use firm, ripe avocadoes.

SERVES 10-12

MEXICAN CHEESE PIZZA

This pizza has a Mexican flavour, and is a nice change from the Italian version. If you don't want to make the base, simply purchase a ready made one. It makes a delicious appetizer.

1 READY MADE PIZZA BASE or HOMEMADE PIZZA DOUGH[1]
375ml (1½ cups) TOMATO SALSA[2]
250ml (1 cup) CHEDDAR or TUSSERS, GRATED
8-10 CALAMATA OLIVES, PITTED
250ml (1 cup) SOUR CREAM
GUACAMOLE

GUACAMOLE
2 MEDIUM AVOCADOES, PEELED AND CUT INTO CHUNKS
½ RED ONION, COARSELY DICED
1 SMALL TOMATO, DICED WITH SKIN
45-60ml (3-4 Tbs) LEMON JUICE
COARSE SALT
CHILLI (IF REQUIRED)

Preheat oven to 180°C (375°F). This can either be baked on a baking tray lined with sprayed foil or on an exopat mat.[3] Spread some salsa on the pizza base. Top with grated cheese and dot with olives. Bake for 20 minutes or until bubbling. Remove from oven. Place spoonfuls of sour cream and dollops of guacamole on top of baked pizza. Serve immediately.

1 See pizza dough recipe for Cheeseless Grilled Veg Pizza.
2 Refer back of book. 3 Specialized baking mat of silicone.

SERVES 8

TOMATO AND MOZZARELLA STACK WITH BASIL CREAM

SMOKED FISH TERRINE

PUMPKIN BREAD

What a gorgeous bread this is! It can almost be eaten as a cake. It can be served with soups or any starter.

250ml (1 cup) TOASTED PEPITAS (PUMPKIN SEEDS)
500ml (2 cups) FLOUR
5ml (1 tsp) BAKING POWDER
5ml (1 tsp) BICARBONATE OF SODA
5ml (1 tsp) SALT
10ml (2 tsps) CINNAMON
5ml (1 tsp) GROUND GINGER
PINCH OF NUTMEG
500ml (2 cups) COOKED PUMPKIN
125ml (1/2 cup) SUGAR
80ml (1/3 cup) TREACLE BROWN SUGAR
80ml (1/3 cup) SUNFLOWER OIL
2 JUMBO EGGS
175ml (3/4 cup) BUTTERMILK, YOGHURT or NON-DAIRY - USE ORLY WITH LEMON JUICE

Preheat oven to 160°C (350°F).

Toast pepitas by placing them on a baking tray in a 140°C (325°F) for 10 minutes. Keep a careful watch over them, as they puff up and pop when they toast. Remove from oven and cool slightly. Keep 1/2 cup aside to sprinkle on top of loaves. Coarsely chop remaining 125ml (1/2 cup) in food processor.

Puree pumpkin. Set aside.

Mix dry ingredients together. Stir sugars and pumpkin together.

Process oil and eggs in food processor with metal blade. Add dry ingredients then pumpkin and pulse to blend. Add buttermilk or yoghurt.

Line a loaf tin 15cm (6 inch) with baking paper. Spray the tin and paper.

Bake bread for about 50 minutes or until well browned. Allow to cool in tin.

NOTE: Bread freezes very well. Reheat if desired.

SERVES 8

ASPARAGUS PHYLLO CRISPS

When you want a drinks party to be a hit, make these. They can be made without the cheese, so use margarine for brushing and season the asparagus well inside the phyllo. Your guests will eat more than you can ever dream of because they are so unusual and so delicious. Ensure you have extras.

36 FRESH GREEN ASPARAGUS
6 SHEETS OF PHYLLO PASTRY
UNSALTED BUTTER FOR BRUSHING
125g (4 oz) CRUMBLED FETA or GRATED PARMESAN

Preheat oven to 180°C (375°F).

Peel the stems of the asparagus with a vegetable peeler.

Brush 1 sheet of phyllo with butter. Cut sheet into 6. Sprinkle a little parmesan or feta down the middle of each square. Place 1 asparagus on each square and roll up phyllo with asparagus top and bottom protruding.

Place on a baking sheet. Brush outside of phyllo with butter. Sprinkle with black pepper.

Bake for 10 minutes before serving. They will keep uncovered on a hot tray.

NOTE: Can be made the day before. Cover well with plastic wrap and keep refrigerated until just before baking. Bake as above. Do not freeze these unbaked.

MAKES 36 ASPARAGUS ROLLS
ALLOW 3 PER PERSON

ASPARAGUS PHYLLO CRISPS

BABY POTATO AND SMOKED SALMON SALAD

A stunning variation of your average potato salad, but even more appealing and just as easy to make. The rich pink of the salmon contrasts with the blandness of the potato and makes a great starter.

30 BABY POTATOES, UNPEELED
500g (1 lb) SMOKED SALMON or SMOKED SALMON OFF-CUTS, CUT INTO STRIPS
60ml ($^1/_4$ cup) CHOPPED CHIVES
1 SMALL RED ONION, FINELY CHOPPED

Boil baby potatoes until firm but cooked. Cut in half lengthwise with the skin on. Allow to cool. Mix with cut salmon strips, chives and red onion.

DRESSING
250ml (1 cup) SWEET MAYONNAISE*
125ml ($^1/_2$ cup) CREAM OR MILK
45ml (3 Tbs) LEMON JUICE
SALT AND PEPPER

Whisk dressing ingredients together.

NOTE: Salad can be prepared ahead and dressed a few hours before.

* See appendix

SERVES 8-10

MARINATED SWEET & SOUR SALMON FILLETS WITH HORSERADISH SAUCE

This is an ingenious way to serve salmon as a cold starter. It is delicious and quite easy to prepare. Serve as a whole fillet of fish on a buffet table or cut into portions and serve with a lovely tossed salad.

1kg (2.2 lbs) NORWEGIAN SALMON FILLET, WITH SKIN ON
1 ONION, SLICED THINLY
250ml (1 cup) WHITE WINE
250ml (1 cup) WHITE VINEGAR
125ml ($^1/_2$ cup) SUGAR
250ml (1 cup) WATER
4 DRY BAY LEAVES
8 BLACK PEPPERCORNS
5ml (1 tsp) SALT

Bring wine, vinegar, sugar, water, bay leaves, peppercorns and salt to a boil. Add sliced onion. Remove pot from stove. Pour liquid into a container. Place salmon fillet, flesh side down in the liquid while it is still hot so that the fillet is covered, to marinate the fish.

HORSERADISH SAUCE
80ml ($^1/_3$ cup) DRAINED RED HORSERADISH*
175ml ($^3/_4$ cup) HELLMANN'S LIGHT MAYONNAISE
60ml ($^1/_4$ cup) CREAM or NON-DAIRY CREAMER

Spoon horseradish sauce over fish before serving.

NOTE: The salmon can be prepared the day before. Cannot be frozen after marinating.

* See appendix

SERVES 4

ZUCCHINI MUFFINS

A lovely change from bran or carrot, these muffins are a nutty combination of sweet and savoury. They are quick and easy to prepare.

2 JUMBO EGGS
125ml ($^1/_2$ cup) SUNFLOWER OIL
125ml ($^1/_2$ cup) TREACLE BROWN SUGAR
500ml (2 cups) COARSELY GRATED ZUCCHINI
500ml (2 cups) FLOUR
2.5ml ($^1/_2$ tsp) BICARBONATE OF SODA
2.5ml ($^1/_2$ tsp) BAKING POWDER
5ml (1 tsp) SALT
5ml (1 tsp) CINNAMON
175ml ($^3/_4$ cup) PLAIN YOGHURT
125ml ($^1/_2$ cup) CHOPPED PECANS

Preheat oven to 180°C (375°F).
Place zucchini in a strainer and salt well. Leave to drain for 20 minutes and then rinse well with cold water. Pat dry. Set aside.

Beat eggs, oil and sugar in mixmaster until creamy. Add grated zucchini, mixed dry ingredients and yoghurt. Beat until just mixed. Stir in pecans.
Spray 12 muffin tins well. Spoon batter into tins almost to the top. Bake on middle rack of oven for 20 minutes or until golden. Test with a toothpick to make sure muffins are baked. Cool in tins and then remove.

NOTE: These freeze very well, and may be reheated for a few minutes just before serving. Muffins bake better when they are not over beaten.

MAKES 12 MUFFINS

BABY POTATO AND SMOKED SALMON SALAD

MARINATED SWEET & SOUR SALMON FILLETS WITH HORSERADISH SAUCE

SPIRAL BREAD

I learnt to make this bread on my travels to Tuscany last year, and it is one of the easiest, tastiest and attractive breads I have made. The spiral shows off the filling.

BREAD DOUGH
200g (7 oz) CAKE FLOUR
30ml (2 Tbs) OLIVE OIL
175ml (3/4 cup) WARM WATER
10g (1 heaped Tbs) INSTANT YEAST
SALT

Mix dry ingredients together. Add olive oil and warm water and mix to form dough. Then knead well until dough is smooth. Place in an oiled bowl, cover with plastic and a cloth and allow to rise for at least 1 hour.

FILLING
1 ONION, FINELY CHOPPED
5ml (1 tsp) MINCED GARLIC (OPTIONAL)
700ml (2 1/2 cups) CRUSHED AND STRAINED TOMATO SAUCE*

STRONG GRATED CHEESE (OPTIONAL) CHEDDAR or HALOUMI

OLIVES AND ANCHOVIES (OPTIONAL)

Sauté onion and garlic in a large pot with a little olive oil. When softened, add strained tomatoes and cook on gentle heat uncovered until very thick (at least 2 hours). Season to taste with sugar, salt and pepper. Allow to cool.

TO ASSEMBLE:

Roll out dough to 1.5 cm (3/4 inch) thickness. Spread with tomato sauce. Top with a little grated cheese, olives and anchovies if desired. Roll up bread and place on exopat mat or baking paper on a baking tray. Make some diagonal slits in the top of the bread. Brush with a little tomato sauce and sprinkle with more cheese.

Bake in preheated 200°C (400°F) oven for 20-30 minutes or until golden.

NOTE: I like to use cake flour for most of my breads. Bread may be reheated very successfully.

*Use whole peeled Italian tomatoes, pureed and strained to get 700ml (2 1/2 cups) of crushed sauce or purchase Italian passata in bottles available in most supermarkets.

SERVES 8

MEZE PLATTER

This is a wonderful idea for starters or hors d'oeuvres, because it feeds a large crowd and it is an easy way of presenting the most stunning looking platter. If you have time to marinate everything yourself, even better, but these days one can buy such wonderful pre-marinated vegetables. Use your imagination! It creates an impressive picture.

CANNED ASPARAGUS SPEARS or FRESH ASPARAGUS (Fresh asparagus: Blanch in boiling water for 3 minutes, then plunge immediately into ice water).

250g (8 oz) MOZZARELLA or TUSSERS CHEESE, THINLY SLICED or BOCCOCINI BALLS.

ROSA CHERRY TOMATOES.

500g (1 lb) FRESH BUTTON MUSHROOMS (Blanch mushrooms in boiling water for 1 minute and then drain well. Place in vinaigrette 2 days before serving) or PURCHASE MARINATED MUSHROOMS.

2 EGGPLANTS, SLICED, SALTED AND GRILLED, THEN MARINATED or READY GRILLED EGGPLANTS.

4 RED, GREEN or YELLOW PEPPERS GRILLED, PEELED & MARINATED or READY MARINATED PEPPERS.

EXTRAS: OLIVES, PEPPADEWS, CHILLIES, FETA, TARAMASALATA, TZATZIKI, HUMMUS, TAHINA, FETA AND HERB DIP, BABY CARROTS, BABY CUCUMBERS.

BABY PITAS or LAFFAH (LEBANESE) BREAD or LARGE PITAS CUT INTO QUARTERS.
(Be sure to put these on last because they will dry out)

ANY GOOD QUALITY ITALIAN SALAD DRESSING FOR MARINATING VEGETABLES or MAKE YOUR OWN.

MARINADE: 60ml (1/4 cup) OLIVE OIL, 30ml (2 Tbs) BALSAMIC VINEGAR, SALT AND PEPPER.

Put all the different vegetables and dips and spreads into small attractive containers on a large platter and decorate with beautiful lettuce packs and fresh herbs.

NOTE: Just remember that if you are not having a large crowd, do not buy large quantities of everything - there's only so much people can eat before a main meal.

SERVES 12-15

MEZE PLATTER

GINGER CARROT SOUP WITH PUMPKIN BREAD (recipe Starters)

Soups

GINGER CARROT SOUP

SPICY NOODLE SOUP

FRESH TOMATO SOUP

CHILLED BEETROOT SOUP

Soups

Soups

I hope that these soups will inspire you because with their different herbs, spices and seasonings, they too are following changing food trends. The combination of textures in some of them will titillate your taste buds.

I have given you specific quantities for stock cubes or powders and these should always be added to boiling water as specified in the recipe. If you are kosher, then always use a pareve chicken stock powder or cube instead of a vegetable cube which contains potato in it and which will thicken your soup unnecessarily. As a rule I prefer to use Knorr or Maggi cubes and powder. If however, you do not like using MSG, which is contained in all these stocks, substitute with Herbamare Natural seasoning or Plantaforce cubes which are natural, or use ready-packed liquid stocks which are completely natural and which are more readily available in most supermarkets worldwide. These require only salt to enhance their natural flavour.

With vegetarianism becoming so much more popular, as cooks we have to be prepared to cater for all guests. These vegetarian soups can be served as hors d'oeuvres or as a main meal, with one of the many wonderful types of bread available either at the store or homemade.

Soups

QUICK AND EASY

- CHICKEN SOUP
- EGGPLANT SOUP
- PEA SOUP
- ZUCCHINI SOUP

RECIPES

- ROASTED RED PEPPER AND TOMATO SOUP
- TWO PEA SOUP
- GINGER CARROT SOUP
- WILD MUSHROOM SOUP EN CROÛTE
- FRENCH VEGETABLE SOUP WITH BASIL PISTOU
- FRENCH ONION SOUP GRATINÉE
- ASPARAGUS VICHYSOISSE
- FRESH TOMATO SOUP
- SPICY NOODLE SOUP
- CHILLED BEETROOT SOUP WITH APPLE SOUR CREAM AND CHOPPED PISTACHIOS

CHICKEN SOUP

1 WHOLE PRE-COOKED CHICKEN, SKINNED AND BONED (USE CHICKEN MEAT ONLY)

50g (2 oz) CAPELLINI or ANGEL HAIR PASTA, UNCOOKED
6 TELMA CHICKEN STOCK CUBES or 3 KNORR CHICKEN STOCK CUBES
ENOUGH COLD WATER TO COVER CHICKEN
15ml (2 Tbs) CHOPPED PARSLEY

Break chicken into big pieces. Cover with water and add stock cubes. Bring to a boil and then simmer with the lid on for $1/2$ hour. Add capellini (or angel hair pasta) and parsley and continue to simmer for another $1/2$ hour. Adjust seasoning.

SERVES 6-8

EGGPLANT SOUP

6 LEEKS, (WHITES ONLY) SLICED
1kg (2.2 lbs) EGGPLANT, PEELED AND CUT INTO PIECES
2 Litres (8 cups) BOILING WATER
90ml (6 Tbs) TELMA PAREVE CHICKEN STOCK POWDER or 3 KNORR VEGETABLE STOCK CUBES or 90ml (6 Tbs) MAGGI VEGETABLE STOCK POWDER

Sauté leeks in olive oil until softened.
Add eggplant, boiling water and stock powder and simmer until softened - about 20 mins. Liquidise.

Add 125ml ($1/2$ cup) cream if desired.

Adjust seasoning.

SERVES 8-10

PEA SOUP

60ml (4 Tbs) BUTTER or MARGARINE
500g (1 lb) PACKET FROZEN PETIT POIS (PEAS), DEFROSTED
1 LETTUCE, SHREDDED AND CHOPPED
4 SPRING ONIONS, CHOPPED
1.1 Litres (5 cups) BOILING WATER
45-60ml (3-4 Tbs) TELMA PAREVE CHICKEN STOCK POWDER or 45ml (3 Tbs) MAGGI VEGETABLE STOCK POWDER
SALT AND PEPPER

FRESH MINT FOR DECORATING

Melt butter or margarine in a large pot. Sauté onions until soft. Add lettuce and peas and cook for about 5 mins. Add stock. Increase heat and bring to a boil. Reduce heat and simmer for approximately 15 minutes.

Purée soup in batches. Adjust seasoning.
Decorate with mint and a drop of cream if desired.

SERVES 8

ZUCCHINI SOUP

80ml ($1/3$ cup) OLIVE OIL
1 LARGE ONION, CHOPPED
750g (1 $1/2$ lbs) ZUCCHINI, CHOPPED
2 LARGE CARROTS
2 LARGE POTATOES, CHOPPED
2 Litres (8 cups) BOILING WATER
60ml (4 Tbs) TELMA PAREVE CHICKEN STOCK POWDER or 90ml (6 Tbs) MAGGI VEGETABLE STOCK POWDER
15ml (1 Tbs) FRESH BASIL

Fry onion in olive oil until softened.

Add zucchini, carrots, potatoes, boiling water and stock powder and simmer over medium heat until vegetables are soft. Add basil and continue to simmer. Liquidise soup.

SERVES 6-8

ROASTED RED PEPPER AND TOMATO SOUP

Roasting these vegetables changes their taste and makes this a stunning soup. It can have a spicy Thai flavour or a simpler natural one.

3 LARGE RED PEPPERS
1 ONION
3 LARGE CARROTS
2 STICKS CELERY (WITH LEAVES)
60ml ($^1/_4$ cup) OLIVE OIL
2.5ml ($^1/_2$ tsp) CHILLI PASTE or POWDER (ADD MORE IF DESIRED)
400g (14 oz) CAN ITALIAN-STYLE SLICED TOMATOES
5 SUN-DRIED TOMATOES IN VINAIGRETTE & 80ml ($^1/_3$ cup) VINAIGRETTE (FROM TOMATOES)*
1 Litre (4 cups) BOILING WATER
60ml (4 Tbs) TELMA PAREVE CHICKEN STOCK POWDER or 45ml (3 Tbs) MAGGI VEGETABLE STOCK POWDER
125ml ($^1/_2$ cup) COCONUT MILK or CREAM (OPTIONAL)

Place peppers on a baking tray directly under the grill and char the skin all over. Cool slightly and then peel skin. Remove seeds under cold running water. Chop coarsely and set aside.

Preheat oven to 200°C (400°F).

Place onion, carrots and celery in food processor and chop coarsely. Place this mixture in a roasting pan, adding olive oil, chilli paste or powder, canned tomatoes, sun-dried tomatoes, vinaigrette, salt and pepper and roast for about 30 minutes uncovered. Add peeled peppers and roast a further 15 minutes.

Cool and place in food processor with vegetable stock powder and water in batches. Process. Adjust seasoning. Add coconut milk or cream if desired. *

NOTE: The coconut milk or the cream will change the taste of the soup completely, but can be omitted if desired. If you like a spicier soup add a little more chilli, if not omit completely as it does have a tang to it. This soup can be made ahead and refrigerated. Reheats beautifully. Freeze without the coconut milk or cream.

* See appendix

SERVES 6-8

TWO PEA SOUP

This is an original combination of vegetables, which transform this soup into an exotic, smooth, tasty delight.

60ml (4 Tbs) MARGARINE or BUTTER
5 LEEKS, WHITE PART ONLY, SLICED THINLY
3 LARGE POTATOES, DICED SMALL
1 Litre (4 cups) FROZEN PETIT POIS (BABY PEAS)
250g ($^1/_2$ lb) SNOW PEAS
CUT INTO A VERY FINE JULIENNE
1.2 Litres (6 cups) BOILING WATER
75ml (5 Tbs) PAREVE CHICKEN STOCK POWDER or 60ml (4 Tbs)
MAGGI VEGETABLE STOCK POWDER
1 ICEBERG LETTUCE, SHREDDED
A FEW MINT LEAVES FOR FLAVOUR
SALT AND PEPPER

Sauté leeks and potatoes with margarine or butter in a large pot. Do not allow to brown.

Add stock and simmer for at least $^1/_2$ an hour or until potatoes are softened.

Add frozen peas and lettuce and $^3/_4$ of snow peas. Add mint leaves. Simmer for another 15 minutes.

Strain out mint leaves. Liquidise entire mixture. Then add remaining snow peas. Adjust seasoning with salt and pepper.

NOTE: This soup does not need any cream. Add a little white pepper if necessary. Freezes very well. Can be made and refrigerated for several days before serving.

SERVES 6-8

ROASTED RED PEPPER AND TOMATO SOUP & SPIRAL BREAD (recipe Starters)

WILD MUSHROOM SOUP EN CROÛTE

Beneath an elegant crust simmers a variety of mushrooms and a hint of curry in a rich broth.

4 MEDIUM LEEKS, SLICED
2 CARROTS, CHOPPED
2 TURNIPS, CHOPPED
60ml (4 Tbs) OLIVE OIL
5ml (1 tsp) MINCED GARLIC
250g (1/2 lb) MEDIUM BROWN MUSHROOMS, SLICED
250g (1/2 lb) PORTABELLINI MUSHROOMS, SLICED
250g (1/2 lb) WHITE BUTTON MUSHROOMS, SLICED
30g (1 oz) DRIED PORCINI MUSHROOMS, SOAKED IN 125ml (1/2 cup) BOILING WATER
2 LARGE POTATOES, DICED
2 Litres (8 cups) BOILING WATER

75ml (5 Tbs) TELMA PAREVE CHICKEN STOCK POWDER or 60ml (4 Tbs) MAGGI VEGETABLE STOCK POWDER
2 BAY LEAVES
5-10ml (1-2 tsps) MILD CURRY POWDER
30ml (2 Tbs) SWEET WINE or PORT
SALT AND PEPPER

1 200g (7 oz) ROLL PUFF PASTRY
1 EGG BEATEN WITH A LITTLE WATER FOR BRUSHING

Sauté leeks, carrots, turnips and garlic in oil until golden.

Add brown, white and portabellini mushrooms and sauté, seasoning with salt and pepper until softened. Chop porcini mushrooms. Add them and their liquid to the soup and then add potatoes, bay leaves and stock and simmer for at least 45 minutes or until potatoes are soft.

Whisk in curry powder. Strain half of mushrooms out of soup. Remove bay leaves. Add sweet wine or Port.

Place remaining soup in food processor and process until quite smooth. Add 5-10ml (1-2 tsps) stock powder should soup need more flavour. Place the saved mushrooms back into the soup.

TO MAKE CRUST: Roll out some puff pastry, ensuring it is not too thin.

Ladle hot soup into small ovenproof containers or one large deep soup bowl.* Brush edge of container with egg and place puff pastry over top pressing edges with a fork. Brush top of puff pastry with egg. Make a very small hole in the top of the pastry to allow steam to escape.

Preheat oven to 220°C (440°F) and bake for 20 mins or until golden.

*NOTE: Deep dish should not be larger than 20cm (8 inch) in diameter or pastry will sag when baking.

This soup is more user friendly when made in individual bowls.

SERVES 8-10

GINGER CARROT SOUP

The rich sweetness of the carrots is balanced by the slight ginger taste that comes through the soup. It is a marvellous blend of sensations.

1 ONION, CHOPPED COARSELY
15ml (1 Tbs) FRESH GINGER
30ml (2 Tbs) MARGARINE or OLIVE OIL
8 CARROTS, GRATED COARSELY or SHREDDED IN FOOD PROCESSOR
2 LARGE SWEET POTATOES, CUT INTO PIECES
2 Litres (8 cups) BOILING WATER
90ml (6 Tbs) TELMA PAREVE CHICKEN STOCK POWDER or 60ml (4 Tbs) MAGGI VEGETABLE STOCK POWDER
5ml (1 tsp) SALT
5ml (1 tsp) SUGAR

Fry onion and ginger in margarine or oil until lightly golden. Add sweet potato and carrots and stir for a few minutes to coat them. Add stock powder and water. Bring to a boil. Reduce heat and simmer with the lid on the pot for at least 1-1/2 to 2 hours to ensure carrots are very soft.

Liquidise entire mixture. Adjust seasoning with stock powder if necessary. Add salt and sugar. If too thick add extra water.

NOTE: Freezes very well.

SERVES 10

WILD MUSHROOM SOUF EN CROÛTE

FRENCH VEGETABLE SOUP WITH BASIL PISTOU

The colourful chopped vegetables and the basil make this soup a sensational all-rounder.

250g ($^1/_2$ lb) DRIED HARICOT BEANS or
410g (14 oz) CAN HARICOT BEANS, DRAINED
10ml (2 tsps) OLIVE OIL
1 ONION, FINELY CHOPPED
2 GARLIC CLOVES, CRUSHED
1 CELERY STALK, CHOPPED
3 CARROTS, DICED
BOUQUET GARNI - BUNCH OF MIXED HERBS TIED TOGETHER WITH STRING*
4 POTATOES, DICED
150g (6 oz) THIN GREEN BEANS, CHOPPED
2 Litres (8 cups) BOILING WATER
90ml (6 Tbs) PAREVE CHICKEN STOCK POWDER or
75ml (5 Tbs) MAGGI VEGETABLE STOCK POWDER
3 TOMATOES, PEELED AND DICED
4 ZUCCHINI, CHOPPED
150g (4 oz) VERMICELLI or VERY THIN PASTA
150g (4 oz) FROZEN PETIT POIS (BABY PEAS) (about 2 cups)

Soak the beans in water overnight and then boil until tender - about 1 hour. (If using canned beans, they don't need soaking, just add them later).

Heat the olive oil in a large pot. Add the onion and garlic and sauté for a few minutes. Add the celery, carrot, bouquet garni and cook for 10 minutes, stirring occasionally. Add the potatoes, green beans, boiling water and stock powder and simmer for another 10 minutes.

Peel the tomatoes and dice. Add to the soup with the zucchini, vermicelli and peas. Simmer for another 15-20 minutes.

BASIL PISTOU
6 GARLIC CLOVES or 10ml (2 tsps) MINCED GARLIC
60g (2 oz) FRESH BASIL LEAVES
125ml ($^1/_2$ cup) FETA or PARMESAN GRATED
250ml (1 cup) OLIVE OIL

Place garlic, basil and parmesan in a food processor and process. Add olive oil in a stream with the motor running. Set aside.

Place a spoonful of pistou in centre of soup in each dish when serving.

*1 sprig each fresh rosemary, oregano, thyme, sage

NOTE: This soup can be made ahead. However, if reheating do not cook vegetables too long initially or they will not retain their colour. Only add pistou when serving. Basil pistou freezes very well.

SERVES 8-10

FRENCH ONION SOUP GRATINÉE

A good, old-fashioned French onion soup topped with oozing melted cheese croutons.

60ml (4 Tbs) MARGARINE
4 ONIONS, SLICED VERY THINLY
1$^3/_4$ Litres (5$^1/_2$ cups) BOILING WATER
4 TELMA PAREVE BEEF or 2 KNORR BEEF CUBES
30ml (2 Tbs) FLOUR
1 BAY LEAF
PINCH OF CRUMBLED DRY THYME
30ml (2 Tbs) BRANDY
8 SLICES FRENCH BREAD
500ml (2 cups) GRATED TUSSERS or EMMENTALER CHEESE
60ml ($^1/_4$ cup) GRATED PARMESAN (OPTIONAL)

Melt margarine. Sauté onions for at least 20 mins or until well browned on medium-high heat. Stir in flour and sauté for another few mins. Add beef stock dissolved in boiling water and stir until thickened. Add bay leaf, thyme and brandy.

Taste for seasoning and add an additional 1 Telma or $^1/_2$ Knorr cube if necessary. Soup must be very rich in taste. Grind some black pepper into soup.

Simmer with lid on for approximately 15 mins.

Preheat oven to 200°C (400°F).

Place bread slices on baking sheet and toast until lightly browned. Sprinkle with Tussers or Emmentaler. Grill until cheese is melted.

Ladle soup into individual bowls. Place 1 slice of toasted bread in each bowl. Sprinkle with parmesan (if desired). Serve immediately.

NOTE: May be refrigerated. Do not freeze.

SERVES 4-6

FRENCH VEGETABLE SOUP WITH BASIL PISTOU

ASPARAGUS VICHYSOISSE

Only fresh green asparagus can give you such a creamy, vibrant low fat soup.

30ml (2 Tbs) MARGARINE or BUTTER
45ml (3 Tbs) OLIVE OIL
2 RED ONIONS OR 3 LEEKS, SLICED
6 MEDIUM POTATOES, PEELED AND DICED
500g (1 lb) FRESH GREEN ASPARAGUS or ZUCCHINI CUT UP
1.5 Litres (6 cups) BOILING WATER
75ml (5 Tbs) PAREVE CHICKEN STOCK POWDER or 60ml (4 Tbs) MAGGI VEGETABLE STOCK POWDER or 3 KNORR CHICKEN STOCK CUBES

CHIVE OIL
1 X 30g (1 oz) PACKET FRENCH CHIVES, CUT INTO SMALL PIECES
80ml (1/3 cup) OLIVE OIL
SALT TO TASTE

In a large pot, melt the butter and add the oil. Sauté the red onions or leeks until softened. Add the potatoes and sauté for a few minutes.

Stir in the stock powder and boiling water and simmer until the potatoes are softened. Just before pureeing, add the asparagus for not more than 3 minutes or they will change the colour of the soup.

Liquidise the entire mixture. Reheat as desired. Drizzle a little chive oil on the top when serving.

CHIVE OIL: Place chives in food processor with the oil and salt and purée until well mixed. Refrigerate until ready to use.

NOTE: Can be made ahead and reheated. Freezes very well. Do not use canned asparagus, as they can be very stringy.

SERVES 6-8

FRESH TOMATO SOUP

A fantastic freshly made, creamy tomato soup.

60ml (4 Tbs) OLIVE OIL
125ml (1/2 cup) CHOPPED CELERY
1 ONION, CHOPPED
125ml (1/2 cup) CHOPPED CARROTS
80ml (1/3 cup) FLOUR
2 X 400g (2 X 14 oz) CANS WHOLE PEELED TOMATOES, CHOPPED WITH LIQUID
15ml (1 Tbs) SUGAR
5ml (1 tsp) DRY BASIL or 15ml (1 Tbs) FRESH BASIL
5ml (1 tsp) DRY MARJORAM
1 BAY LEAF
1 Litre (4 cups) BOILING WATER
60ml (4 Tbs) PAREVE CHICKEN STOCK POWDER or
45ml (3 Tbs) MAGGI VEGETABLE STOCK POWDER
125ml (1/2 cup) CREAM or RICH'S NON-DAIRY MILK*
250ml (1 cup) MILK or RICH'S NON-DAIRY MILK
2.5ml (1/2 tsp) PAPRIKA
2.5ml (1/2 tsp) MILD CURRY POWDER
DROP OF WHITE PEPPER
SALT TO TASTE

Heat oil in a large pot. Sauté celery, onion and carrots until tender. Stir in flour and cook for 2 mins. Add tomatoes, sugar, basil, marjoram, bay leaf, boiling water and stock powder. Cover and simmer for 30 mins stirring occasionally. Discard bay leaf.

Purée in batches in food processor or liquidiser. Add cream, milk, paprika, curry powder and pepper. Stir well. Season with salt.

May be served hot or cold.

NOTE: Can be refrigerated and frozen without the cream. Should you not be able to obtain Rich's non-dairy cream, rather omit it entirely, or you will spoil the soup.

* See appendix

SERVES 6-8

ASPARAGUS VICHYSOISSE

SPICY NOODLE SOUP

You can choose your level of spice and heat, but you will definitely wow your guests with this one.

PASTE
4 THICK STALKS LEMONGRASS
30ml (2 Tbs) FRESH GINGER
1 LARGE ONION
5ml (1 tsp) CHILLI PASTE (OPTIONAL)
10ml (2 tsps) MINCED GARLIC
12 MACADAMIA NUTS (OPTIONAL)
60ml (1/4 cup) WATER
30ml (2 Tbs) SUGAR
80ml (1/3 cup) OIL

2 Litres (8 cups) BOILING WATER
6 TELMA or 4 KNORR CHICKEN STOCK CUBES
4 CHICKEN BREASTS, SKINLESS AND BONELESS
125g (4 oz) CAPELLINI NOODLES, PRE-BOILED
1 BLOCK TOFU, CUT INTO SMALL CHUNKS (OPTIONAL)
CORIANDER LEAVES FOR DECORATING

Place lemongrass, ginger, onion, chilli paste, garlic, macadamias, water, sugar and oil in a food processor and process until it forms a paste.

Simmer chicken breasts in stock for about 1/2 an hour. Strain soup and remove chicken. Set aside and when cool, shred finely.

Place paste in a pot and sauté until it starts to bubble. Allow it to turn a slightly darker brown and bubble again for a few minutes. Add strained stock to pot. Then place shredded chicken back into soup. Simmer gently.

Boil noodles in a pot of boiling water. Place a mound of noodles in each bowl. Top with soup and add tofu. Sprinkle with a few coriander leaves for decoration.

SERVES 6-8

CHILLED BEETROOT SOUP WITH APPLE SOUR CREAM AND CHOPPED PISTACHIOS

An exotic combination of textures and tastes, the crunchy pistachios contrast with the smoothness of the soup. Although not normally a lover of cold soups, this is one of my favourites.

500g (1 lb) WHOLE BEETROOT, PEELED AND CUT INTO QUARTERS
4 LARGE CARROTS, PEELED AND CUT INTO CHUNKS
15ml (1 Tbs) FRESH GINGER, CHOPPED FINELY
45ml (3 Tbs) OLIVE OIL
175ml (3/4 cup) TREACLE BROWN SUGAR
10ml (2 tsps) SALT
30ml (2 Tbs) FRESH LEMON JUICE
5ml (1 tsp) TELMA PAREVE CHICKEN STOCK POWDER or MAGGI VEGETABLE STOCK POWDER
BLACK PEPPER
1 Litre (4 cups) COLD WATER

Preheat oven to 180°C (375°F).

Place beetroot and carrots in a small roasting pan. Sprinkle with ginger, olive oil, sugar, salt, pepper and stock powder. Cover with foil and roast for 40-50 minutes or until beetroot are softened. Allow to cool.

Place roasted vegetable mixture into food processor with some cold water, lemon juice and salt to taste and process with metal blade until finely chopped and smooth. Set aside in a bowl and add remaining water. Adjust seasoning.

APPLE SOUR CREAM SAUCE
250ml (1 cup) SOUR CREAM or PLAIN YOGHURT
250ml (1 cup) APPLE SAUCE

Whisk apple sauce together with sour cream (or yoghurt).

250ml (1 cup) SHELLED PISTACHIOS, TOASTED AND CHOPPED

NOTE: This soup keeps very well for up to a week in the refrigerator. Add additional water if too thick. Should you prefer a more savoury soup, reduce the quantity of sugar when roasting beetroot.

TO SERVE: Refrigerate soup and serve chilled. Top with a dollop of apple sour cream mixture and sprinkle with some pistachios.

SERVES 6-8

SPICY NOODLE SOUP

CHILLED BEETROOT SOUP WITH
APPLE SOUR CREAM AND CHOPPED PISTACHIOS

SASHIMI SALMON SALAD

Salads

SASHIMI SALMON SALAD

FESTIVE SALAD

ISLAND SALAD

MEXICAN TORTILLA SALAD

Salads

Salad

In the past few years, we have moved from the traditional salads, to more exotic combinations of vegetables, salads and dressings. It is not uncommon today to add fruit and nuts to our salads as well as meat, chicken and fish. The dressings have also undergone a transformation from the usual vinegary, salty type to fruity, nutty and even spicy ones.

In keeping with this trend I have included many wonderful and different salads which you will really enjoy. Many of the dressings can be made well ahead of time.

Remember that natural sea salt always brings out the flavour in a dressing and freshly ground black pepper adds to the taste. Never use a strong olive oil as it will overpower all other tastes. Salads should only be dressed just before serving as specified in the recipe, and try to serve your salad chilled as it keeps all the vegetables and fruit fresh and crisp.

Salads

QUICK AND EASY

- CURRIED PINEAPPLE SALAD
- CUCUMBER AND FETA SALAD
- LETTUCE SALAD WITH LIME MAYONNAISE
- MARINATED CABBAGE SALAD

RECIPES

- BABY SPINACH, TOMATO AND STRAWBERRY SALAD
- MIXED ASIAN SALAD
- MEXICAN TORTILLA SALAD
- STRAWBERRY AND ALMOND SALAD
- SEARED BEEF SALAD
- SASHIMI SALMON SALAD
- LAYERED ROASTED VEGETABLE SALAD WITH TAHINA DRESSING
- ISLAND SALAD
- CARAMELISED PEAR AND ALMOND SALAD
- GRILLED HALOUMI SALAD WITH TZATZIKI
- FESTIVE SALAD
- SHAVED FETA, ASPARAGUS AND MUSHROOM SALAD
- TOASTED BARLEY, CHICKPEA AND CARROT SALAD
- MINTED BABY POTATO AND PEA SALAD

CURRIED PINEAPPLE SALAD

1 BUTTER LETTUCE
300g (9.5 oz) PACKET BABY SPINACH
440g (15 oz) CANNED PINEAPPLE PIECES, DRAINED WELL
100g (3.5 oz) SLIVERED ALMONDS
3 SPRING ONIONS, THINLY SLICED
1 AVOCADO, THINLY SLICED

DRESSING
2.5ml (1/2 tsp) GARLIC SALT
125ml (1/2 cup) OIL
80ml (1/3 cup) WHITE WINE VINEGAR
30ml (2 Tbs) TREACLE BROWN SUGAR
10ml (2 tsps) MILD CURRY POWDER
15ml (1 Tbs) SOYA SAUCE
SALT AND PEPPER

Toast the almonds on a baking tray in a preheated 140°C (325°F) oven.

In a bowl, make layers of butter lettuce, spinach, pineapple pieces, almonds, spring onions and avocadoes.

Whisk all dressing ingredients together and pour over salad just before serving. Toss lightly just before serving.

NOTE: Assemble salad several hours ahead. Pour dressing over just before serving.

SERVES 6-8

CUCUMBER AND FETA SALAD

1 ENGLISH CUCUMBER SLICED THINLY, WITH SKIN
200g (7 oz) CRUMBLED FETA

DRESSING
60ml (4 Tbs) FRESHLY CHOPPED OREGANO
60ml (1/4 cup) OLIVE OIL
JUICE OF 1 LEMON
SALT AND PEPPER

Slice cucumber thinly and layer on a flat platter, alternating with crumbled feta.
Drizzle dressing over and allow to marinate for a little while. Taste for seasoning.

SERVES 6-8

LETTUCE SALAD WITH LIME MAYONNAISE

250g (4 oz) SMOKED SALMON, SMOKED SALMON TROUT or OFF-CUTS (OPTIONAL)
1 ICEBERG LETTUCE
1 HEAD BUTTER LETTUCE

DRESSING
250ml (1 cup) SWEET MAYONNAISE*
60ml (1/4 cup) LIME CORDIAL
5ml (1 tsp) PAPRIKA
2.5ml (1/2 tsp) CHILLI PASTE or POWDER
1-2 HARD BOILED EGGS, FINELY CHOPPED
SALT AND PEPPER

Whisk dressing ingredients together and add hard-boiled eggs.

Cut lettuces in half. Place attractively on a platter. Pour dressing over just before serving. Mound strips of smoked salmon in the centre of the platter.

* See appendix

SERVES 6

MARINATED CABBAGE SALAD

2 GREEN CABBAGES
1 BUNCH SPRING ONIONS, THINLY SLICED (WITH GREEN)

MARINADE
375ml (1 1/2 cups) WHITE WINE VINEGAR or APPLE CIDER VINEGAR
250ml (1 cup) OLIVE OIL
175ml (3/4 cup) SUGAR
125ml (1/2 cup) VEGETABLE STOCK POWDER*
17.5ml (1 1/2 Tbs) SALT
17.5ml (1 1/2 Tbs) DRY MUSTARD POWDER
17.5ml (1 1/2 Tbs) CELERY SEEDS

Heat marinade ingredients in a small pot to dissolve sugar on low heat. Remove from stove.
Shred cabbages very finely and layer with spring onion in alternate layers in a glass bowl.

Pour dressing over cabbages and onion.
Allow to marinate for a few hours before serving.

* Kosher - use Pareve Telma Chicken Stock Powder

SERVES 8

LETTUCE SALAD WITH LIME MAYONNAISE

BABY SPINACH, TOMATO AND STRAWBERRY SALAD

I love this salad because the roasting of the cherry tomatoes offsets the sweetness of the strawberries and contrasts with the crunchy fried onion rings.

300g (9.5 oz) BABY SPINACH, LEAVES BROKEN
200g (7 oz) ROSA CHERRY TOMATOES, CUT IN HALF
500g (½ lb) SMALL STRAWBERRIES
2 ONIONS, CUT INTO THICK ROUNDS AND FRIED

Cut cherry tomatoes in half and place in a small roasting pan. Season generously with salt and pepper and drizzle with olive oil. Place in a preheated 200°C (400°F) oven and roast uncovered for about 10 minutes. Remove and cool.

Heat a little oil in a frying pan (about 2 cm - ⅘ inch deep). Dip onion rings into beaten egg and then quickly into flour and lightly fry in oil until golden. Drain on paper towel. Do not cover.

TO ASSEMBLE: Place baby spinach on platter. Top with tomatoes and strawberries and lastly with the onion.

DRESSING
30ml (2 Tbs) PAPINO SEEDS*
10ml (2 tsps) MUSTARD POWDER
80ml (⅓ cup) SUNFLOWER OIL
80ml (⅓ cup) OLIVE OIL
60ml (¼ cup) APPLE CIDER or RICE VINEGAR
30ml (2 Tbs) TREACLE BROWN SUGAR
½ ONION
SALT AND PEPPER

Place all ingredients in food processor and process until as smooth as possible. Taste and adjust for seasoning.

Just before serving, drizzle dressing over salad.

* Scoop only papino seeds from inside of papino.

SERVES 6-8

MIXED ASIAN SALAD

An exciting eastern-influenced salad with a creamy dressing

500g (1 lb) MEDIUM BROWN MUSHROOMS, GRILLED
500g (1 lb) FRESH ASPARAGUS, GRILLED

100g (7 oz) FLAKED ALMONDS, TOASTED
100g (7 oz) PINE NUTS, TOASTED

RED ONION (IF AVAILABLE), SLICED THINLY

1 BUTTER LETTUCE

DRESSING
60ml (¼ cup) SWEET MAYONNAISE*
30ml (2 Tbs) APPLE CIDER VINEGAR or RICE VINEGAR
30ml (2 Tbs) WHITE WINE VINEGAR
30ml (2 Tbs) SOYA SAUCE
15ml (1 Tbs) HONEY
5ml (1 tsp) GROUND GINGER
10ml (2 tsps) SESAME OIL
5ml (1 tsp) CHILLI PASTE or 1ml (¼ tsp) CHILLI POWDER
60ml (¼ cup) OLIVE OIL

Preheat oven to 220°C (440°F).

Place mushrooms in a roasting pan and drizzle with a little olive oil. Season with salt and pepper and roast until quite dry - about 20 mins. Set aside. Allow to cool.

Place asparagus in same pan and grill directly under the grill for 2 minutes, drizzled with olive oil and seasoned with salt and pepper. Allow to cool.

Whisk all dressing ingredients together. Place mushrooms in dressing a few hours before serving to allow them to marinate.

Break up butter lettuce on a platter. Remove mushrooms from the marinade, slice thickly and place on top of lettuce. Arrange asparagus on salad. Scatter with red onions. Drizzle with dressing and top with toasted nuts.

TO TOAST NUTS: Place on a baking sheet on 140°C (325°F) for 10 minutes until golden.

* See appendix

SERVES 8

BABY SPINACH, TOMATO AND STRAWBERRY SALAD

MEXICAN TORTILLA SALAD

A stunning, make-ahead, layered salad with a tangy, pink dressing that seeps through the vegetable layers. Crunchy tortilla chips complement both taste and texture.

1 ICEBERG LETTUCE, SHREDDED
3 TOMATOES, DICED AND DRAINED
1 ENGLISH CUCUMBER, SEEDED AND DICED
2 AVOCADOES, DICED
2 MIELIES, CORN REMOVED [or 250ml (1 cup) CANNED CORN]
4 SPRING ONIONS, COARSELY CHOPPED
375ml (1 1/2 cups) GRATED CHEDDAR or TUSSERS CHEESE

1 LARGE PACKET TORTILLA CHIPS OR BIG KORN BITES

DRESSING
175ml (3/4 cup) CHUNKY SALSA (MILD)*
60ml (1/4 cup) TOMATO JUICE
60ml (1/4 cup) OLIVE OIL
15ml (1 Tbs) LEMON JUICE
30ml (2 Tbs) SOUR CREAM or YOGHURT
15ml (1 Tbs) CHOPPED CORIANDER
2.5ml (1/2 tsp) CAYENNE PEPPER or CHILLI PASTE
SALT AND PEPPER

Whisk all ingredients for dressing together and refrigerate until ready to use.

Layer lettuce, tomatoes, cucumber, avocadoes, spring onions and mielies (corn) in a glass bowl. Top with grated cheese.

Pour over dressing half an hour before serving. Top with crushed tortilla chips just before serving.

NOTE: Drain tomatoes very well before layering in salad. Do not dice vegetables too small, or you will not have enough volume.

* See appendix

SERVES 10-12

STRAWBERRY AND ALMOND SALAD

A colourful display of red and green - sweet and savoury.

250g (8 oz) FRESH GREEN ASPARAGUS, GRILLED
2 BUTTER LETTUCES, BROKEN INTO PIECES
250g (8 oz) STRAWBERRIES, HALVED
125ml (1/2 cup) FLAKED ALMONDS TOASTED
30ml (2 Tbs) POPPY SEEDS
30ml (2 Tbs) TOASTED SESAME SEEDS

DRESSING
125ml (1/2 cup) WHITE SUGAR
2.5ml (1/2 tsp) PAPRIKA
60ml (1/4 cup) WHITE WINE VINEGAR*
60ml (1/4 cup) APPLE CIDER VINEGAR
125ml (1/2 cup) OLIVE OIL

Toast almonds and sesame seeds on a baking tray in a 140°C (325°F) oven for 10 minutes or until golden. Allow to cool.

Whisk all dressing ingredients together, allowing sugar to dissolve.

Arrange lettuce, strawberries, almonds, poppy seeds and sesame seeds on platter. Top with dressing just before serving.

* If kosher white wine vinegar is not available, use a double quantity of apple cider vinegar.

SERVES 6

MEXICAN TORTILLA SALAD

STRAWBERRY AND ALMOND SALAD

SEARED BEEF SALAD

A wonderful salad where leftover rare beef can be used. Crispy noodles and a light balsamic dressing offset this delightful picture.

1 X 1 kg (2.2 lbs) SCOTCH FILLET or RUMP STEAK or FILLET
200g (7 oz) MIXED LETTUCE (2 packets)
200g (7 oz) ROSA CHERRY TOMATOES
$\frac{1}{2}$ SLICED ENGLISH CUCUMBER

MARINADE FOR MEAT
60ml (4 Tbs) SOYA SAUCE
5ml (1 tsp) GROUND CORIANDER
30ml (2 Tbs) OLIVE OIL
30ml (2 Tbs) BALSAMIC VINEGAR
10ml (2 tsps) SUGAR

Mix all ingredients together and pour over meat. Allow to marinate for at least 2-3 hours or longer, turning meat during marinating.

Preheat oven to 200°C (400°F). Pour off marinade and roast meat uncovered on both sides for:

SCOTCH FILLET - 40 mins
FILLET - 15 mins
RUMP STEAK - Sear in a very hot frying pan on both sides until meat is rare.

All the meat should be rare before carving. Slice thinly and place in the centre down the length of the platter. Surround with the lettuces, tomatoes and cucumber.

DRESSING
125ml ($\frac{1}{2}$ cup) OLIVE OIL
80ml ($\frac{1}{3}$ cup) BALSAMIC VINEGAR
30ml (2 Tbs) SOYA SAUCE
30ml (2 Tbs) TREACLE BROWN SUGAR
2.5ml ($\frac{1}{2}$ tsp) GINGER
SALT AND PEPPER

Whisk all ingredients for dressing together and drizzle over salad just before serving.

Sprinkle with crispy noodles.

CRISPY FRIED NOODLES - Boil 125g (4 oz) thin noodles until just cooked. Drain and dry very well. Heat a little oil in a frying pan and when hot fry noodles until crispy and golden. Drain on paper towel. Crush a little before sprinkling over platter.

SERVES 6-8

SASHIMI SALMON SALAD

Ever popular sushi ingredients have been included to make this salad light, fresh and japaneasy.

100g (3.5 oz) PACKET MIXED LETTUCE
$\frac{1}{4}$ ENGLISH CUCUMBER, PEELED AND JULIENNED
1 CARROT, FINELY JULIENNED
1 SPRING ONION, FINELY SLICED
250ml (1 cup) BEAN SPROUTS
$\frac{1}{2}$ AVOCADO CUT INTO FINE STRIPS
30ml (2 Tbs) TOASTED SESAME SEEDS

SALMON SASHIMI - 12 SLICES

DRESSING
125ml ($\frac{1}{2}$ cup) OLIVE OIL
45ml (3 Tbs) SUGAR
60ml ($\frac{1}{4}$ cup) FRESH LIME JUICE or BOTTLED LEMON JUICE
2.5ml ($\frac{1}{2}$ tsp) CHILLI PASTE or POWDER
30ml (2 Tbs) SOYA SAUCE
2.5-5ml ($\frac{1}{2}$ - 1 tsp) WASABI POWDER (OPTIONAL)*
SALT AND PEPPER

Whisk all dressing ingredients together, ensuring that sugar dissolves before dressing salad.

Toss lettuce with most of the dressing. Place on a platter. Sprinkle with cucumber, carrot, spring onions, bean sprouts and avocado. Drizzle with remaining dressing.

Arrange fish pieces on top attractively. Sprinkle with sesame seeds.

Serve immediately.

NOTE: Dressing can be made ahead and refrigerated. The salad can be made without the fish.

* See appendix

SERVES 4-6

SEARED BEEF SALAD

LAYERED ROASTED VEGETABLE SALAD WITH TAHINA DRESSING

This may be time-consuming, but the wow factor is immeasurable. Be sure to make extra!

ALL VEGETABLES ARE SLICED PAPER-THIN LENGTHWISE AND NOT PEELED:

2 SWEET POTATOES
6-8 BABY POTATOES
6 LARGE ZUCCHINI
¼ - ½ BUTTERNUT
2 EGGPLANTS (DO NOT NEED SALTING)

DRESSING
30ml (2 Tbs) LEMON JUICE
45ml (3 Tbs) OLIVE OIL
55ml (3 heaped Tbs) TAHINA*
(ready made sesame sauce)
PINCH OF CAYENNE PEPPER
PINCH OF PAPRIKA
SALT AND PEPPER

Preheat oven to 220°C (440°F).

Place vegetables individually on exopat mat* or lightly oiled foil on a baking tray and brush them with a little olive oil. Season with salt and bake on middle rack until browned. Turn over and continue baking until vegetables are crispy, golden and almost dry. Repeat procedure until all vegetables are baked.

Place on open platters or baking trays and keep uncovered and separate to prevent them from becoming soggy. Cool completely.

TO SERVE: Arrange vegetables in long rows in alternate layers directly on a platter. Drizzle with dressing just before serving.

NOTE: Dressing can be made ahead. Do not dress until just before serving or vegetables will become soggy. Vegetables must be made the day you serve the salad. Do not refrigerate.

* See appendix

SERVES 6-8

ISLAND SALAD

Raw beetroot tops a mound of vegetables, that are drenched in a fruity mango dressing to make this both a very colourful and delectable salad.

200g (7 oz) MIXED LETTUCE
250g (8 oz) FRESH GREEN ASPARAGUS, PEELED AND BLANCHED
½ RED PEPPER, CUT INTO STRIPS
1 RED ONION, SLICED THINLY
1 CARROT, JULIENNED
200g (7 oz) RAW BUTTERNUT, JULIENNED
2-3 RAW BEETROOT, JULIENNED
200g (7 oz) BABY CUCUMBER, CUT INTO RIBBONS
200g (7 oz) ROSA CHERRY TOMATOES

DRESSING
1 RED ONION, CUT UP
45ml (3 Tbs) BALSAMIC VINEGAR
60m (¼ cup) OLIVE OIL
250ml (1 cup) MANGO PURÉE*
2.5ml (½ tsp) GROUND GINGER
SALT AND PEPPER

Place all dressing ingredients in food processor. Process until onion is chopped.
Season generously with salt and pepper for flavour.

SALAD: Mound lettuce in centre of platter. Arrange vegetables in spokes around the lettuce. Top the mound of lettuce with julienned beetroot. Place cucumber ribbons at the base of lettuce and dot with rosa cherry tomatoes.

Spoon dressing around base and on top of salad just before serving.

NOTE: Dressing can be made 1-2 days ahead and refrigerated.

* Use canned mangoes, drained to obtain purée when mangoes are out of season, or freeze fresh mangoes pureed in season, in plastic bags until ready to use.

SERVES 6-8

LAYERED ROASTED VEGETABLE SALAD WITH TAHINA DRESSING

ISLAND SALAD

CARAMELISED PEAR AND ALMOND SALAD

A light mustard dressing glazes sticky, sweet pears and almonds atop butter lettuce.

1 BUTTER LETTUCE, BROKEN
1 COS LETTUCE, BROKEN
2 AVOCADOES, SLICED
$^1/_2$ ENGLISH CUCUMBER, SLICED THINLY
1 RED ONION, SLICED THINLY

4 FIRM PEARS, SLICED THINLY (WITH SKIN)
250ml (1 cup) SLIVERED or FLAKED ALMONDS
30ml (2 Tbs) MARGARINE or BUTTER
125ml ($^1/_2$ cup) SUGAR
80ml ($^1/_3$ cup) WATER

Melt margarine or butter in a large frying pan. Add sliced pears and almonds and sauté until slightly golden.

Then add sugar and water stirring continuously. Allow this mixture to caramelise on medium - high heat. When golden, remove from heat. Do not remove before caramel becomes golden enough or it will not be sticky.

Place pears and almonds on an exopat mat* or sprayed foil and separate them before they cool or they will harden and stick together. Cool.

DRESSING
60ml ($^1/_4$ cup) FINELY CHOPPED RED ONION
125ml ($^1/_4$ cup) OLIVE OIL
60ml ($^1/_2$ cup) WHITE WINE VINEGAR or
APPLE CIDER VINEGAR
15ml (1 Tbs) WHOLEGRAIN or DIJON MUSTARD*
30ml (2 Tbs) HONEY
SALT AND PEPPER

Whisk all ingredients together, adding chopped red onion. Drizzle over salad just before serving.

TO ASSEMBLE: Place lettuces on a platter. Arrange avocado, cucumber and red onion slices on top and around lettuces. Arrange pear slices and almonds on top. Drizzle with dressing and serve.

* See appendix

SERVES 6-8

GRILLED HALOUMI SALAD WITH TZATZIKI

A fresh salad in both texture and taste, with the tartness of the lemon balancing the saltiness of the haloumi. The tzatziki adds a traditional Greek touch.

500g (16 oz) HALOUMI CHEESE*
100g (3.5 oz) PACKET MIXED LETTUCES
1 ICEBERG LETTUCE
$^1/_2$ ENGLISH CUCUMBER, SLICED
2-3 TOMATOES, SLICED
1 RED ONION, SLICED
1 AVOCADO, SLICED

DRESSING
125ml ($^1/_2$ cup) OLIVE OIL
45ml (3 Tbs) FRESH LEMON JUICE
5ml (1 tsp) MUSTARD POWDER
2.5ml ($^1/_2$ tsp) SUGAR
SALT AND PEPPER

Whisk all dressing ingredients together and set aside. Slice haloumi into finger-size slices and heat a non-stick frying pan on medium-high.

Spray pan with a little olive oil cooking spray. Fry sliced haloumi on both sides until golden. Set aside on an ovenproof plate until ready to use or keep warm in a low 120°C (300°F) oven.

Toss salad ingredients with dressing just before serving and arrange attractively on a flat platter. Place grilled cheese slices around edge of platter on the side of the salad. Serve immediately with extra wedges of lemon and tzatziki.

TZATZIKI
1 ENGLISH CUCUMBER, PEELED AND SEEDED
175ml ($^3/_4$ cup) PLAIN YOGHURT
10ml (2 tsps) FRESH LEMON JUICE
2.5ml ($^1/_2$ tsp) MINCED GARLIC (IF DESIRED)
SALT AND PEPPER

Peel and seed an English cucumber. Grate coarsely. Place in a colander and salt liberally. Allow to stand for 10-15 mins to allow excess liquid to drain. Rinse with cold water and squeeze until quite dry.

Mix together with yoghurt, lemon juice to taste, salt, pepper and garlic (optional).

* Haloumi cheese can become rubbery when it cools. It needs to be served warm, so if you have made it in advance, it can be placed on a plate and reheated in the microwave on high power for 1-2 minutes, but it must be served immediately thereafter. If you are making this for a large crowd, reheat the cheese in batches in order to prevent it getting cold and rubbery.

SERVES 6

CARAMELISED PEAR AND ALMOND SALAD

FESTIVE SALAD

This salad conjures up images of tropical islands with its green, red and orange, sweet and crunchy colours and textures.

2 CARROTS, JULIENNED
300g (9.5 oz) BABY SPINACH, BROKEN
2 BABY RED CABBAGES, SHREDDED FINELY
1 RED ONION, THINLY SLICED
200g (7 oz) RAW BUTTERNUT, JULIENNED
250ml (1 cup) GLACÉED PINEAPPLE PIECES
250ml (1 cup) PEPITAS (PEELED PUMPKIN SEEDS) TOASTED*

DRESSING
30ml (2 Tbs) SOYA SAUCE
45ml (3 Tbs) APPLE CIDER VINEGAR
5ml (1 tsp) CHOPPED CHIVES or SPRING ONIONS
80ml (1/3 cup) OLIVE OIL
SALT AND PEPPER

Whisk all dressing ingredients together.

Mix spinach, cabbage, carrots, red onion and butternut together in a bowl.

Toss with the dressing just before serving and then sprinkle glacéed pineapple and pumpkin seeds around and on top of salad.

* Toast pumpkin seeds on a baking tray in a 180°C (375°F) oven until they puff.

SERVES 8-10

SHAVED FETA, MARINATED ASPARAGUS AND MUSHROOM SALAD

Layers of paper-thin salty feta complement a medley of vegetables and colours.

250g (8 oz) FETA, CUT INTO PAPER THIN SLICES
1 SMALL RED PEPPER, GRILLED, PEELED AND SLICED*
1 SMALL YELLOW PEPPER, GRILLED, PEELED AND SLICED*
410g (14 oz) CAN GREEN ASPARAGUS CUTS, DRAINED
500g (1 lb) WHITE MUSHROOMS, BLANCHED FOR 1 MIN. AND COOLED, THEN QUARTERED
2 SPRING ONIONS, FINELY CHOPPED
30ml (2 Tbs) FRESHLY CHOPPED PARSLEY

BUTTER LETTUCE FOR LINING PLATTER

DRESSING
125ml (1/2 cup) OLIVE OIL
125ml (1/2 cup) SUNFLOWER OIL
125ml (1/2 cup) WHITE WINE VINEGAR
10ml (2 tsps) SALT
10ml (2 tsps) DIJON or WHOLEGRAIN MUSTARD*
7.5ml (1 1/2 tsps) SUGAR
PEPPER

Whisk all dressing ingredients together.

Slice peppers and place in a Tupperware with other vegetables, excluding feta. Pour dressing over at least 2 days before serving to allow them to marinate.

Just before serving, turn out onto a bed of butter lettuce and top with shaved feta.

NOTE: Grill peppers until charred on all sides. Place in a plastic bag. Then place under cold water and remove seeds and skin. Cut into slices

* See appendix

SERVES 6-8

FESTIVE SALAD

TOASTED BARLEY, CHICKPEA AND CARROT SALAD

An unusual, healthy assortment of uncommon ingredients makes this a very colourful, tasty salad.

125ml (1/2 cup) BARLEY, TOASTED
375ml (1 1/2 cups) BOILING WATER
25ml (1 1/2 Tbs) TELMA PAREVE CHICKEN STOCK POWDER or 15ml (1 Tbs) MAGGI VEGETABLE STOCK POWDER
410g (14 oz) CAN CHICKPEAS, DRAINED
1 COS LETTUCE, COARSELY SHREDDED
300g (9 1/2 oz) FRESH SPINACH, COARSELY SHREDDED
4 TOMATOES DICED
2 CARROTS, JULIENNED

Lightly toast the dry barley in a small pot on medium heat until golden but not burnt.

Then add vegetable stock and simmer with lid on for about 30-45 minutes or until soft and liquid has evaporated. Barley should be nutty in flavour and taste.

Mix lettuce and spinach together. Mound on a platter. Surround with tomatoes and carrots.

Place barley around the base of the lettuce/spinach on platter.

Spoon chickpeas onto the centre of the mound and around the sides.

Drizzle with dressing just before serving.

DRESSING
500ml (2 cups) FRESH CARROT JUICE
30ml (2 Tbs) FRESH LEMON JUICE
45ml (3 Tbs) OLIVE OIL
7.5ml (1 1/2 tsps) GROUND CUMIN
5ml (1 tsp) SALT
FRESHLY GROUND BLACK PEPPER

Whisk all ingredients together.

NOTE: Assemble salad before serving and only dress about half an hour before.

SERVES 6-8

MINTED BABY POTATO AND PEA SALAD

This is a delicious combination of warm potatoes with a creamy hint of mint in the dressing. The green peas make an outstanding contrast to the mushrooms.

30 BABY POTATOES, WITH SKIN
500g (1 lb) WHITE MUSHROOMS, WHOLE
4 TOMATOES
4 LEEKS (WHITES ONLY) SLICED AND FRIED
250ml (1 cup) FROZEN PETIT POIS

DRESSING
80ml (1/3 cup) OLIVE OIL
60ml (1/4 cup) WHITE WINE VINEGAR or APPLE CIDER VINEGAR
15ml (1 Tbs) MUSTARD POWDER
10ml (2 tsps) CASTOR SUGAR
125ml (1/2 cup) YOGHURT or SOUR CREAM
SALT AND PEPPER
Whisk all the dressing ingredients

Preheat oven to 200°C (400°F).

Cut potatoes in half and place in a roasting pan. Drizzle with olive oil and season with salt and pepper. Roast for 30 mins. tossing occasionally. Add mushrooms after 30 minutes and 30ml (2 Tbs) chopped mint. Season and roast for another 20 minutes.

Remove and allow to cool.

Lightly fry the leeks to soften them.

Keep potatoes and mushrooms warm and add dressing, leeks and peas (defrosted) just before serving.

SERVES 8-10

TOASTED BARLEY, CHICKPEA AND CARROT SALAD

GRILLED SALMON BURGERS

Fish

GRILLED SALMON BURGERS

THAI FISH CURRY

STIR-FRY FISH WITH VEGETABLES

MARINATED FETA FISH

Fish

Fish is versatile, healthy, low fat and lends itself to any type of flavour. I love using high heat methods as this brings out the colour and retains the moisture and the taste.

Linefish varies all over the world. I like ones that are non-fishy but firm, and my favourites are local Kabeljou and Cape Salmon, as they tend to remain moist. In Australia the equivalent would be Cod or Snapper, whilst in the US, Halibut, Sea Bass and Whitefish. Salmon has many different names, but is essentially the same all over the world and contains excellent Omega 3 fatty acids. Due to its fatty nature it is a much richer fish, so it can naturally be eaten in smaller quantities.

A very good rule-of-thumb for most fish, except salmon, is 10 minutes per 1cm (1/3 inch) of thickness at the thickest part of the fish. Following this rule will always produce perfectly cooked fish. Salmon, however, requires less time and should always be slightly under cooked when removed from the heat, otherwise it tends to dry out.

Recipes are varied ranging from stir-frying to grilling to roasting, but in all these methods, the fish is best when cooked just before serving.

QUICK AND EASY

- HONEY-MUSTARD GLAZED FISH
- GRILLED TERIYAKI SALMON
- KINGKLIP IN LEMON YOGHURT SAUCE
- OVEN-CRISPED FISH FILLETS

RECIPES

- RUSSIAN FISH PIE
- ROASTED FISH STEAKS WITH VEGETABLES
- GRILLED SALMON BURGERS
- STIR-FRY FISH WITH VEGETABLES
- THAI FISH CURRY
- COUSCOUS CRUSTED FISH WITH AVOCADO SALSA
- BAKED FISH STRUDELS WITH TOMATO SAUCE
- FISH FILLETS WITH RED PEPPER PURÉE
- SEARED SALMON ON TARTARE MASH
- WHOLE POACHED FISH WITH DILL SAUCE
- POACHED LINEFISH WITH POTATOES, SPINACH AND TARRAGON SAUCE
- WHOLE STUFFED FISH WITH HONEY-LIME SAUCE
- GRILLED FISH WITH HORSERADISH SAUCE
- MARINATED FETA FISH

Fish

HONEY-MUSTARD GLAZED FISH

1kg (2.2 lbs) KINGKLIP or LINEFISH FILLETS
30ml (2 Tbs) OLIVE OIL
SALT, PEPPER AND HERBAMARE

SAUCE
125ml (1/2 cup) WHOLEGRAIN MUSTARD
30ml (2 Tbs) HONEY
30ml (2 Tbs) SOYA SAUCE
SALT AND FRESHLY GROUND BLACK PEPPER

Mix all sauce ingredients together.

Preheat grill in oven.

Brush fish with half the sauce and place on a foil-lined baking tray. Season with salt, pepper and herbamare. Grill for 10 mins on middle rack of oven until brown.

Turn fish over, brush other side with sauce, season and place under grill again for a further 10-15 mins or until golden.

SERVES 4

GRILLED TERIYAKI SALMON

6 X 200g (7 oz) SALMON FILLETS, SKIN ON

SAUCE
125ml (1/2 cup) SOYA SAUCE
60ml (1/4 cup) COLD WATER
5ml (1 tsp) GARLIC SALT
30ml (2 Tbs) TREACLE BROWN SUGAR
SALT AND PEPPER

Place all sauce ingredients in a small pot and heat gently to dissolve the sugar. Cool slightly before pouring over fish. Cover a baking tray with foil and spray well with non-stick cooking spray. Spoon a little sauce onto the foil. Place fillets, skin side down on the sauce. Pour remaining sauce over the fish. Season with salt and pepper.

Preheat grill in oven. Place rack just under the grill. Grill until well browned - about 5-8 minutes.
Serve immediately.

SERVES 6

KINGKLIP IN A LEMON YOGHURT SAUCE

1kg (2.2 lb) KINGKLIP FILLET

SAUCE
125g (8 Tbs) BUTTER or MARGARINE
5ml (1 tsp) SALT
30ml (2 Tbs) LEMON JUICE
5ml (1 tsp) MAIZENA (CORNSTARCH)
250ml (1 cup) PLAIN YOGHURT
45ml (3 Tbs) FRESH DILL, CHOPPED or
10ml (2 tsps) DRY DILL
SALT AND FRESHLY GROUND BLACK PEPPER

Preheat oven to 220°C (425°F).

Melt the butter in a medium pot over a low heat. Whisk in the salt, pepper and lemon juice. Stir the maizena, yoghurt and dill together and whisk into the butter and lemon juice mixture. Heat gently, do not boil.

Place fish in a lightly greased baking dish and pour over sauce. Bake for 20-25 mins. basting continuously, or until fish is just cooked. Serve immediately.

SERVES 4

OVEN-CRISPED FISH FILLETS

1kg (2.2 lbs) HAKE, KINGKLIP, KABELJOU or CAPE SALMON FILLETS, SKINNED
160ml (2/3 cup) FLOUR
15ml (1 Tbs) HERBAMARE (or OTHER SEASONING)
250ml (1 cup) TOASTED BREAD CRUMBS or KELLOGGS CORNFLAKE CRUMBS
SALT AND PEPPER

2 EGGS, BEATEN

Preheat oven to 220°C (440°F).

Dip fish into flour well-seasoned with herbamare, salt & pepper, then into beaten egg and lastly into toasted crumbs. Place coated fish on sprayed foil or an exopat mat on a baking tray. Spray crumbed fish with olive oil spray. Bake 20 minutes on middle rack of oven. If fish needs to be browned, turn on grill for a few minutes.

Squeeze lots of fresh lemon juice over just before serving with steamed vegetables or roasted sweet potatoes.

SERVES 4-6

RUSSIAN FISH PIE

You will thoroughly enjoy making this delicious fish pie, with its simple flavours and delicate sauce.

500g (1 lb) KINGKLIP or HAKE CUBES (or MIXTURE OF BOTH)

6 SHEETS PHYLLO
1 ONION, CHOPPED
60g (4 Tbs) BUTTER
30ml (2 Tbs) FLOUR
250ml (1 cup) MILK
JUICE OF 1 SMALL LEMON
5 SPRING ONIONS, CHOPPED
15ml (1 Tbs) CHOPPED PARSLEY
1 EGG BEATEN
SALT AND PEPPER
OLIVE OIL SPRAY

Sauté onion in butter until golden. Stir in flour and cook 1 minute before adding the milk. Then whisk until sauce thickens. Season well with salt and pepper. Stir in lemon juice, spring onions and parsley. Then add fish. Stir gently until fish becomes opaque and the mixture thickens slightly. Allow to cool.

Preheat oven to 180°C (375°F).

Line a baking tray with sprayed foil or an exopat mat. Spray 6 sheets of phyllo with olive oil spray. Stack one on top of the other.

Brush the top sheet with beaten egg. Place fish filling in centre on the long side of the phyllo. Roll up to make a loose strudel, pinching sides together. Brush outside of strudel with more egg and spray with more olive oil spray. Sprinkle with some chopped parsley.

Bake for 30-35 mins. Serve with sauce.

SAUCE
160ml (2/3 cup) SOUR CREAM or YOGHURT
80ml (1/3 cup) MAYONNAISE
5ml (1 tsp) LEMON RIND
10ml (2 tsps) LEMON JUICE
SALT AND PEPPER

Whisk all ingredients together. Do not heat sauce.

NOTE: Strudel can be prepared in advance, covered with plastic wrap and refrigerated until ready to use. Bring to room temperature before baking.

SERVES 8-10

ROASTED FISH STEAKS WITH VEGETABLES

This makes a glorious display of colour and taste. The simplicity of olive oil and lemon juice brings out the wonderful taste of the fresh fish.

6 NORWEGIAN SALMON or LINEFISH STEAKS (KABELJOU or CAPE SALMON)
2 RED ONIONS, SLICED AND LIGHTLY BROWNED

200g (7 oz) ROSA CHERRY TOMATOES, HALVED
500g (16 oz) BUTTON MUSHROOMS, HALVED
250g (8 oz) SNOW PEAS, HALVED
(or ASPARAGUS IN SEASON)
OLIVE OIL
COARSE SALT, HERBAMARE AND BLACK PEPPER
JUICE OF 2 LEMONS
GRATED RIND OF 1 LEMON

Preheat oven to 240°C (450°F).

Drizzle a little olive oil into a large roasting pan. Set aside.

Lightly fry red onions in a little olive oil until browned and place in roasting pan. Season fish very well on both sides and place on top of onions. Scatter tomatoes, mushrooms and snow peas on top of fish. Drizzle with a drop more oil. Sprinkle generously with coarse salt and pepper.

SALMON: Place on bottom rack of preheated oven and cook for 8 mins. Turn over and check seasoning. Sprinkle with lemon juice and rind. Bake for another 5-7 mins. Remove from oven and serve immediately.

LINEFISH: Place on bottom rack and cook for 10 mins. Turn over, check seasoning and sprinkle with lemon juice and rind. Bake 10 mins on the other side. Serve immediately.

TO SERVE: Place a fish steak on each plate and surround with vegetables.

NOTE: It is advisable to add the lemon juice and rind halfway through the cooking process as they will give the fish more flavour.

SERVES 6

ROASTED FISH STEAKS WITH VEGETABLES

GRILLED SALMON BURGERS

These are a firm favourite in my family because they are not fried, nor do they have much oil. The wonderful colour from the salmon peeks through the cakes.

250g (8 oz) MINCED HAKE
300g (9 oz) SALMON FILLET, SKINNED

1 ONION, DICED
30ml (2 Tbs) OLIVE OIL
RIND OF 1 LEMON
JUICE OF 1 LEMON
HANDFUL CHOPPED PARSLEY
30ml (2 Tbs) WHOLE GRAIN MUSTARD
1 EGG YOLK
SALT AND PEPPER

2 EGG WHITES

1 MEDIUM POTATO, PEELED AND PARBOILED UNTIL SOFT - COARSELY DICED

Cut the salmon fillet into small pieces. Set aside.

Fry the onion in olive oil until softened and golden and place in food processor. Add the minced hake, lemon rind, lemon juice, chopped parsley, mustard, egg yolk, salt and pepper and process until well mixed.

Add the potato and salmon and pulse until just mixed through.

In a separate bowl, whisk the egg whites until stiff and then fold into the fish mixture. Season very well.

Heat a non-stick frying pan or grilling pan on medium-high. Drizzle a drop of olive oil into the pan or spray with olive oil spray.

Place large, flat spoonfuls of fish mixture into the pan in the shape of a burger and grill until well browned on one side.

Turn over gently with a spatula and grill the other side until cooked completely.

Serve with some chunky chopped avocado and/or lemon wedges.

MAKES 12 MEDIUM BURGERS

STIR-FRY FISH WITH VEGETABLES

A wonderful combination of vegetables, fish and noodles. The fish must be firm or it will break when stir-frying.

250g (8 oz) PRE-COOKED LINGUINE

1kg (2.2 lbs) KINGKLIP (or ANY VERY FIRM FISH), CUT INTO STRIPS
60ml (1/4 cup) FLOUR
SALT AND PEPPER
OLIVE OIL

Heat a wok with a little olive oil. Dip fish pieces lightly into well-seasoned flour and quickly sear on all sides to seal the juices. Remove and place on paper towel until ready to use. Clean wok and continue.

4 SPRING ONIONS, DIAGONALLY SLICED
5ml (1 tsp) MINCED GARLIC or 1 GARLIC CLOVE, CRUSHED
1/2 RED PEPPER, CUT INTO THIN STRIPS
1/2 YELLOW PEPPER, CUT INTO THIN STRIPS
1 CARROT, JULIENNED
250g (8 oz) MUSHROOMS, SLICED AND PRE-FRIED
300g (9 1/2 oz) BOK CHOY, THICKLY SLICED

Heat a little more olive oil in the wok until very hot, but not smoking.
Quickly stir-fry mushrooms until all excess liquid has evaporated. Remove and set aside.

SAUCE
200ml (2/3 cup) SUN-DRIED TOMATO SAUCE*†
45ml (3 Tbs) SOYA SAUCE
30ml (2 Tbs) HONEY
SALT AND PEPPER

Mix all sauce ingredients together. Pour into the wok and boil on high until well reduced and thickened.

Add the spring onions, garlic, peppers, carrot and cooked mushrooms to the sauce and stir-fry for 1 min. Place prepared fish back in the wok. Add bok choy and quickly stir-fry for a minute to complete cooking.

Serve immediately on a bed of linguine.

* I use Ina Paarman Coat and Cook Sun-dried Tomato Sauce, but any comparable strong flavoured one will do.
† See sauces

SERVES 6-8

STIR-FRY FISH WITH VEGETABLES

THAI FISH CURRY

A sensational combination of fish and red curry paste that will make your mouth water. Serve on a bed of steamed jasmine rice.

1kg (2.2 lbs) KINGKLIP or OTHER FIRM FISH FILLETS

125ml (1/2 cup) FLOUR
SALT AND PEPPER
OIL FOR FRYING

Preheat shallow oil in a frying pan.
Cut fish into thin strips for stir-frying. Dip into seasoned flour. Fry very quickly on both sides to sear and brown fish, but not to cook through completely. Set aside to drain on paper towel.

SAUCE
45ml (3 Tbs) HOMEMADE RED CURRY PASTE*
or 15ml (1 Tbs) BOTTLED RED CURRY PASTE
375ml (1 1/2 cups) COCONUT MILK or CREAM
45ml (3 Tbs) TREACLE BROWN SUGAR
5ml (1 tsp) SOYA SAUCE

Whisk sauce ingredients together.

Heat a wok on high and add sauce. Bring to a boil and simmer until sauce is reduced and thickened. Return fried fish to the wok and toss to coat and complete the cooking process.

Serve immediately.

* See appendix

SERVES 4-6

COUSCOUS CRUSTED FISH WITH AVOCADO SALSA

I love making this fish because the couscous gives it a crunchy crust, and it is then baked and topped with a fresh salsa.

1kg (2.2 lbs) LINEFISH, FILLETED AND SKINNED
COARSE SALT CRUSHED
45ml (3 Tbs) OLIVE OIL

1 EGG, BEATEN

250ml (1 cup) COUSCOUS
250ml (1 cup) WHITE WINE
2.5ml (1/2 tsp) SAFFRON or TURMERIC

Bring wine to a boil and add the saffron or turmeric. Add couscous and remove from stove. Stir well and cover with the lid. Leave to steam in pot for 10 minutes. Fluff with a fork until ready to use.

Preheat oven to 200°C (400°F).

Season fish well. Dip into beaten egg.

Then dip into the steamed couscous, coating well all over. Place on a pre-sprayed foil or on an exopat mat on a baking tray. Drizzle with the olive oil. Season again.
Bake for 20-25 minutes. Serve immediately with the salsa.

SALSA
2 AVOCADOES, FINELY CHOPPED
1/2 SMALL ONION, VERY FINELY CHOPPED
2 TOMATOES, CHOPPED
LEMON JUICE
1 TBS OLIVE OIL
SALT AND PEPPER

Toss all ingredients together.

SERVES 4

THAI FISH CURRY

BAKED FISH STRUDELS WITH TOMATO SAUCE

A sensational combination of fish and phyllo, which is completed by the slightly Asian-flavoured tomato sauce.

6 X 250g (8 oz) PORTIONS LINEFISH (SKIN OFF)
250ml (1 cup) WHOLEGRAIN MUSTARD
30ml (2 Tbs) HONEY
30g (1 oz) FRESH DILL, CHOPPED
30g (1 oz) FRESH CHIVES, CHOPPED
30g (1 oz) FRESHLY CHOPPED PARSLEY
SALT, PEPPER
8 SHEETS PHYLLO
OLIVE OIL SPRAY

Preheat oven to 200°C (400°F). Line a baking tray with baking paper or an exopat mat. Set aside.

Stir honey into mustard. Season fish pieces very well, and brush with a little mustard mixture on both sides.

In a small bowl, mix together herbs, salt and pepper Set aside. Spray 4 sheets of phyllo with olive oil spray and place one on top of the other.

Cut the sheets in half down the middle. Turn so long side faces you. You will now have 2 rectangles of phyllo each containing 4 sheets. Sprinkle the top sheet with a little of the herb mixture.

Place 1 fish portion on each phyllo rectangle. Fold in the sides and then roll to enclose the fish and make a strudel. Spray outside of strudels with olive oil spray, sprinkling with more herbs and placing seam side down on prepared baking tray.

Repeat procedure with remaining 4 portions of fish and phyllo. Bake uncovered for 20 minutes. Drizzle with sauce. Serve immediately.

If preparing the fish ahead of time, cover the phyllo well with plastic wrap and refrigerate until ready to bake. Remove an hour before baking to bring to room temperature. It must be baked at such a high temperature to avoid making its own juices whilst baking. Do not use frozen fish, as it oozes during baking and makes the phyllo soggy.

TOMATO SAUCE
60ml (1/4 cup) OLIVE OIL
10ml (2 tsps) CHOPPED GINGER or GINGER PASTE
10ml (2 tsps) CHOPPED SPRING ONION or CHIVES
5ml (1 tsp) MINCED GARLIC
30ml (2 Tbs) SUGAR
400g (14 oz) CAN CHOPPED TOMATOES (WITH JUICE)
15ml (1 Tbs) TOMATO PASTE
30ml (2 Tbs) FRESH LIME JUICE
30ml (2 Tbs) SUNDRIED TOMATO PESTO or PASTE *
125ml (1/2 cup) CREAM (OPTIONAL)
SALT AND PEPPER

In a medium pot, sauté the ginger, spring onions, garlic and sugar in the olive oil until softened. Add the tomatoes and continue to cook on low heat until softened and reduced. Add the tomato paste, lime juice and pesto. Season to taste. Stir in cream and heat for a few minutes on medium to reduce and thicken sauce.

NOTE: The sauce can be made a few days ahead and reheated on low.

NOTE: This dish can be made with 1 large fish fillet, following the same procedure except do not cut the phyllo.

* See appendix

SERVES 6

WHOLE POACHED FISH WITH DILL SAUCE

A perfectly cooked fish with this simple method of poaching, requiring no special equipment. The dill sauce makes the perfect partner.

2kg (4.5 lb) WHOLE NORWEGIAN SALMON or LINEFISH, BUTTERFLIED, WITH HEAD AND TAIL
250ml (1 cup) WHITE WINE
500ml (2 cups) WATER
125ml (1/2 cup) BOTTLED LEMON JUICE
1 LEMON, SLICED
SALT AND PEPPER

Preheat oven to 200°C (400°F).
Line a roasting pan with heavy foil and spray well with non-stick cooking spray.
Season inside of fish well with salt and pepper and line with slices of lemon.

Pour white wine, water and lemon juice around fish and enclose with foil, ensuring that it is completely sealed.

Bake on middle rack of oven for 30 minutes. Remove and prick with a fork to ensure that it is 90% cooked (it will finish cooking while it cools). Reseal foil.

Allow fish to cool, make a small hole in the foil on the underneath side of the fish to drain off excess liquid. Then lift foil, fold back the edge and gently slide fish on to a platter.

Serve at room temperature with dill sauce.

DILL SAUCE
30g (1 oz) FRESH DILL
30ml (2 Tbs) WHITE VINEGAR
30ml (2 Tbs) SUGAR
250ml (1 cup) SWEET MAYONNAISE*
125ml (1/2 cup) CREAM or NON-DAIRY CREAMER

Place all above ingredients in a food processor and process until combined. Refrigerate until ready to use.

NOTE: The fish is best served at room temperature because the flesh does not firm too much. Should you refrigerate the fish, remove from fridge about 2 hours before serving to bring to room temperature.

* See appendix

SERVES 8-10

BAKED FISH STRUDELS WITH TOMATO SAUCE

SEARED SALMON ON TARTARE MASH

I am unlucky to have a family with expensive taste in food who love salmon. The simplicity of this dish is in the cooking and seasoning.

1kg (2.2 lbs) SALMON FILLETS, SKIN REMOVED, CUT INTO 5 PORTIONS
30ml (2 Tbs) OLIVE OIL

30g (1 oz) CHIVES
125ml ($^1/_2$ cup) CHOPPED PARSLEY
SALT, PEPPER, PAPRIKA

Mix chives and parsley together in a bowl. Set aside.

Heat a non-stick pan with some of the olive oil until very hot.

Roll portions of salmon in chive-parsley mixture to coat all sides. Season very well with salt, pepper and paprika. Sear both sides of salmon in batches in frying pan, using balance of olive oil. Remove and place fish on sprayed foil or an exopat mat on a baking tray.

Preheat the oven to 240°C (450°F).

Roast fish on the middle rack of the oven for 8-10 minutes, depending on the thickness of the fish.

45ml (3 Tbs) BUTTER, SOFTENED, MIXED WITH SOME PARSLEY AND CHIVES

Place a drop of parsley/chive butter on each piece of fish just before serving.

Serve with tartare mash potato (recipe Vegetables)

NOTE: The ultimate salmon to use for this particular dish would be Scottish Salmon because of its fatty texture, which suits this method of cooking best. However, a very fresh Norwegian or Canadian salmon will also cook perfectly. Remember that the salmon should always be a little rare when removing from the oven.

SERVES 4

FISH FILLETS WITH RED PEPPER PURÉE

We love pan-fried fish because it is so succulent. The small quantity of butter simply turns the fish to a golden colour, and the sauce is a perfect partner.

1kg (2.2 lbs) KABELJOU, FILLETED AND SKINNED
30ml (2 Tbs) BUTTER
SEASONING - HERBAMARE OR PEPPER

SAUCE
175ml ($^3/_4$ cup) WHITE WINE
125ml ($^1/_2$ cup) ONION, FINELY CHOPPED
5ml (1 tsp) MINCED GARLIC
2 RED PEPPERS, ROASTED AND PEELED
200g (3 oz) BABY CARROTS, COOKED
10ml (2 tsps) SALT
60ml ($^1/_4$ cup) MAYONNAISE
PINCH OF CAYENNE PEPPER
5ml (1 tsp) VEGETABLE or PAREVE CHICKEN STOCK POWDER
BLACK PEPPER

Combine wine, onion and garlic and bring to a boil in a medium pot. Boil until reduced to about 60ml ($^1/_4$ cup).

Purée roasted peppers in food processor until smooth. Add reduced sauce to peppers. Then add carrots, salt, mayonnaise, cayenne pepper, stock powder and black pepper. Process until smooth. Set aside. Reheat when ready to use.

Brown butter in a frying pan. Season fish very well and pan-fry on medium heat until golden on both sides and cooked through. Drizzle sauce over fish just before serving.

SERVES 4

SEARED SALMON ON TARTARE MASH (recipe Vegetables)

POACHED LINEFISH WITH POTATOES, SPINACH AND TARRAGON SAUCE

A juicy fish fillet rests on a bed of potatoes, spinach and tarragon

1.5kg (3 lbs) FRESH LINEFISH FILLET, WITH SKIN ON - KABELJOU, CAPE SALMON or NORWEGIAN SALMON
500ml (2 cups) WATER
JUICE OF 1 LEMON
COARSE SALT

Preheat oven to 200°C (400°F).

Place fish fillet on a double layer of sprayed foil, shiny side of foil up, in a roasting pan. Pour water, lemon juice and salt over fish. Close foil and seal well.

Bake linefish for 20-25 mins and salmon for 15 mins.

8-10 BABY POTATOES, PEELED, sliced lengthwise and boiled in salted water.

300g (9.5 oz) BABY SPINACH
OLIVE OIL
SALT AND PEPPER

Heat a little olive oil in a pan. Chop spinach coarsely and sauté very quickly over high heat, seasoning with salt and pepper.

TO SERVE: Cut fish into serving size portions. Spoon the spinach on to the platter. Top with sliced potatoes and then fish. Spoon sauce over fish just before serving.

SAUCE
30g (1 oz) FRESH CHIVES, FINELY CHOPPED
125ml (1/2 cup) PARSLEY
125ml (1/2 cup) FRESH TARRAGON or
60ml (1/4 cup) DRY TARRAGON
250ml (1 cup) MAYONNAISE*
80ml (1/3 cup) APPLE CIDER VINEGAR or RICE VINEGAR
15ml (1 Tbs) WHOLEGRAIN or DIJON MUSTARD
SALT AND PEPPER TO TASTE

Place all ingredients in a food processor and process until quite smooth. Set aside until ready to use. Sauce can be made and refrigerated for a few days before using.

* See appendix

SERVES 6

WHOLE STUFFED FISH WITH HONEY-LIME SAUCE

The colourful vegetables and noodles peek out from the side of the salmon keeping it moist. This is then topped with a sublime sauce.

1.5kg (3.3 lb) NORWEGIAN SALMON, BUTTERFLIED, SKIN ON

100g (3 oz) FINE NOODLES

30ml (2 Tbs) FRESH GINGER, FINELY CHOPPED
6 SPRING ONIONS, FINELY CHOPPED
1 CARROT, FINELY CHOPPED
250g (8 oz) MUSHROOMS, COARSELY CHOPPED & PRE-FRIED*
30ml (2 Tbs) CORIANDER or PARSLEY, CHOPPED
30ml (2 Tbs) TREACLE BROWN SUGAR
60ml (1/4 cup) SOYA SAUCE
SALT AND PEPPER
OLIVE OIL

Preheat oven to 200°C (400°F).

Break noodles and boil them until just cooked. Mix with the ginger, spring onions, carrot, mushrooms, coriander, sugar and soya. Stuff mixture inside salmon, seasoning insides of fish well with salt and pepper before closing.

Tie the salmon together with string at intervals to enclose the filling. Rub the outside of fish with olive oil and season well.

Place the fish on a foil-lined baking spray, sprayed with olive oil spray. Bake for 20-25 mins or until just cooked through. Remove from oven and cool slightly, removing string before serving

HONEY-LIME SAUCE
125g (4 oz) SALTED BUTTER
60ml (1/4 cup) LIME JUICE
45ml (3 Tbs) SOYA SAUCE
45ml (3 Tbs) HONEY

Melt butter over high heat until brown. Remove from heat and add lime juice, soya and honey. Pour over hot fish just before serving.

* Mushrooms should be fried first to remove excess liquid.

SERVES 6

WHOLE STUFFED FISH WITH HONEY-LIME SAUCE

GRILLED FISH WITH HORSERADISH SAUCE

Sometimes fish needs to be served at room temperature for the best flavour to emerge, because when it is too hot the true taste does not come through.

1.2kg (1 $^{1}/_{2}$ lbs) SALMON or LINEFISH FILLET, WITH SKIN ON

375ml (1 $^{1}/_{2}$ cups) HELLMANN'S LIGHT MAYONNAISE*
125ml ($^{1}/_{2}$ cup) BOTTLED RED HORSERADISH, VERY WELL DRAINED
45ml (3 Tbs) HONEY
30ml (2 Tbs) SOYA SAUCE
30ml (2 Tbs) BOTTLED LEMON JUICE
SALT AND PEPPER TO TASTE

Stir all ingredients together. Set aside.

Preheat grill in oven. Line a baking tray with foil and spray the foil with olive oil spray.
Brush some sauce onto the foil. Place fish skin side down on top of the sauce.

Spread remaining sauce onto flesh side of fish, and season with salt and pepper.

Grill fish in middle of oven until well browned, watching carefully to prevent burning. Do not turn fish. To test readiness, pierce with a fork, which should slide through easily. If not cooked completely, turn oven down to 220°C (425°F) and continue baking for a further 5-10 mins or until cooked through.

Allow to cool on the baking tray. Gently lift foil off baking tray and use the foil to slide fish on to a serving platter. Serve at room temperature.

NOTE: Salmon requires no more than 10-12 minutes cooking time. It must only be grilled for required time and should be slightly under cooked when finished.

* It is important to use a creamy mayonnaise, which will retain the moisture whilst cooking, and coat the fish properly.

SERVES 4

MARINATED FETA FISH

Sometimes a simple fish dish flavoured with herbs and feta brings out its Greek origins and complements it perfectly.

2kg (4$^{1}/_{2}$ lbs) LINEFISH - CAPE SALMON or KABELJOU FILLETS
250ml (1 cup) FRESH LEMON JUICE
60ml ($^{1}/_{4}$ cup) OLIVE OIL
30ml (2 Tbs) FRESH OREGANO or 10ml (2 tsps) DRY OREGANO
5ml (1 tsp) MINCED GARLIC
60ml (4 Tbs) MELTED BUTTER
SALT AND PEPPER

250-500g (1-2 cups) FETA, FINELY CRUMBLED

Marinate fish fillets in a baking dish in the lemon juice, olive oil, oregano, garlic, butter, salt and pepper for at least 1-2 hours before cooking

Preheat grill. Place rack in middle of oven.

Cover entire surface of fish with feta just before grilling. Do not turn fish over. Grill for 20-25 mins. watching that fish does not burn.
Serve immediately.

SERVES 8

GRILLED FISH WITH HORSERADISH SAUCE WITH ROASTED POTATO WEDGES (recipe Vegetables)

TAGLIATELLE AI FUNGHI

Pasta

TAGLIATELLE AI FUNGHI

LEMON AND ASPARAGUS PENNE

SPICY SPAGHETTI ALLA PUTTANESCA

FARFALLE WITH SPINACH

Pasta

We used to associate pasta dishes with warm winter nights, creamy sauces and fat bellies. However, this is not always true because pastas have become the "in-thing" to eat, as they are only as heavy as the sauces with which they are made.

Certain sauces suit some pasta better than others, as they are either too heavy or too light for the actual pasta. But one thing that is apparent is that there are many wonderful and different sauces for the variety that are available today. Always buy a very good quality Italian pasta, as these are lighter than the local kind.

It is essential to boil pasta in a large pot of water, with a handful of kosher or coarse salt added. The pasta can then move freely around the pot and will not stick together. Stir it whilst boiling to prevent it from sticking. Drain immediately before serving and tossing with the sauce. It is better to stir the drained pasta into the heated sauce in the pot or pan, because it can then be tossed together more easily.

If you have the opportunity to learn how to make fresh pasta using a pasta machine, you are in for a treat, because you will really understand the meaning of a wonderful, light, homemade egg pasta. The dough is simply a mixture of eggs and flour (with a little olive oil), kneaded and rolled through the pasta machine until paper thin, then cut and boiled for a very short time (unlike box pasta which takes much longer).

These recipes are a superb mixture of vegetarian dishes, which, combined with delicious bread and a salad make the most sumptuous meal.

Pasta

QUICK AND EASY

- ROSMARINO WITH VEGETABLES
- MACARONI PIZZA
- BASIC TOMATO BASIL SAUCE

RECIPES

- TAGLIATELLE AI FUNGHI
- PENNE WITH TOMATO-HERB SAUCE
- POTATO GNOCCHI WITH ROASTED CHERRY TOMATOES AND SAGE
- MIXED SQUASH GNOCCHI WITH SAGE OIL
- FUSILLI WITH ASPARAGUS CREAM SAUCE
- LEMON AND ASPARAGUS PENNE
- SPICY SPAGHETTI ALLA PUTTANESCA
- ROASTED BUTTERNUT AND ROSEMARY LASAGNE
- FARFALLE WITH SPINACH
- RIGATONI WITH ZUCCHINI SAUCE AND GREMOLATA
- LOW FAT SPINACH AND VEGETABLE LASAGNE

ROSMARINO WITH VEGETABLES

I love this rice-shaped pasta (sometimes called "orzo"), because it is very light and looks exactly like rice. When you add the vegetables, you have a very colourful dish.

150g (5 oz) ROSMARINO, PRECOOKED
2 TELMA PAREVE CHICKEN STOCK CUBES or
15ml (1 Tbs) MAGGI VEGETABLE STOCK POWDER
250ml (1 cup) BROCCOLI HEADS (FRESH or FROZEN)
150g (5 oz) FRESH ASPARAGUS, CUT INTO PIECES
2 TOMATOES, SKINNED, SEEDED AND DICED or
1 RED PEPPER
1 MIELIE (CORN), CUT OFF COB
(or frozen-approx. 125ml ($^1/_2$ cup)
HERBAMARE, SALT AND PEPPER

Boil rosmarino in a large pot of water with some vegetable stock (or pareve chicken stock) added for flavour.

Just before pasta is finished cooking, add vegetables except for tomato and cook with pasta for 2 minutes, and then drain saving a little of the stock.

Season pasta and vegetables very well with lots of herbamare and black pepper. Add tomatoes, and a little stock for taste. Serve immediately.

NOTE: Broccoli and asparagus only need a few minutes to cook.

SERVES 6-8

MACARONI PIZZA

250g (8 oz) MACARONI, COOKED
300g (9 oz) CHEDDAR, GRATED
3 EGGS
175ml ($^3/_4$ cup) MILK
5ml (1 tsp) SALT
PEPPER
80ml ($^1/_3$ cup) TOMATO SAUCE
1 X 400g (14 oz) CAN WHOLE PEELED TOMATOES, CHOPPED AND DRAINED
5ml (1 tsp) DRY BASIL
5ml (1 tsp) DRY OREGANUM

250g (8 oz) MOZZARELLA or TUSSERS, GRATED

Preheat oven to 180°C (375°F).

Boil macaroni and drain. Toss with grated cheddar cheese while warm.

Beat together the eggs, milk, salt and pepper. Pour over the pasta and stir in a bowl to combine. Spread macaroni mixture on to a pizza plate or quiche dish 28cm (11 inch).

In a medium pot heat the tomato sauce, tomato and herbs and simmer to thicken.

Spread tomato mixture over macaroni, sprinkle with grated Mozzarella or Tussers and bake for 20-25 minutes or until golden.

SERVES 8

BASIC TOMATO BASIL SAUCE

1 ONION, CHOPPED FINELY
80ml ($^1/_3$ cup) OLIVE OIL
2 x 400g (14 oz) CANS WHOLE PEELED TOMATOES, CHOPPED WITH LIQUID
30ml (2 Tbs) SUGAR (or MORE IF REQUIRED)
125ml ($^1/_2$ cup) CREAM (OPTIONAL)
30ml (2 Tbs) FRESH BASIL or
10ml (2 tsps) DRY BASIL
SALT AND PEPPER

Fry onion in olive oil until soft and golden.
Add the tomatoes.

Cook over medium-low heat uncovered for half an hour to an hour until thickened.
Add sugar, basil, salt and pepper. Stir in cream if desired.

Can be frozen and reheated.

MAKES 1$^1/_2$ - 2 CUPS

TAGLIATELLE AI FUNGHI

A magical sauce which captures the essence of mushroom flavours.

375g (12 oz) TAGLIATELLE or FETTUCINE

30ml (2 Tbs) BUTTER
30ml (2 Tbs) OLIVE OIL
250g (8 oz) MUSHROOMS, SLICED
250g (8 oz) PORTABELLINI, SLICED (firm brown mushrooms)
3-4 LARGE FRESH PORCINI MUSHROOMS, SLICED*
45ml (3 Tbs) ITALIAN PARSLEY, CHOPPED
250ml (1 cup) WHITE WINE
375ml (1 1/2 cups) STOCK [1 1/2 Tbs PAREVE CHICKEN OR MAGGI VEGETABLE STOCK POWDER DISSOLVED IN BOILING WATER]
60-80ml (1/4 - 1/3 cup) CREAM (IF DESIRED)
SALT AND PEPPER

Melt the butter and oil in a medium pot. Add the chopped parsley and sauté for a few minutes. Add the mushrooms, salt and pepper. Sauté gently over medium heat, stirring all the time. When softened, pour in the wine and reduce by half.

Then add the stock and continue to boil on medium heat uncovered for another 20 minutes.
Taste and adjust seasoning, adding more salt and pepper if necessary. Add cream (if desired).

Boil the pasta until "al dente" just before serving. Heat the sauce and when the pasta has been drained, add it to the sauce, tossing gently to mix through. Serve immediately.

NOTE: The sauce can be made ahead and reheated.

* If fresh porcini are unavailable, soak 20g (1/2 oz) dry porcini in 125ml (1/2 cup) boiling water and add this to the mushrooms and sauce, when porcini are softened.

SERVES 4-6

PENNE WITH TOMATO-HERB SAUCE

The taste that is created by sautéing the herbs first makes this a special tomato sauce for any type of pasta.

500g (16 oz) PENNE, PRE-COOKED

2 CLOVES GARLIC or 5ml (1 tsp) MINCED GARLIC
1 ONION, CHOPPED
1 SPRIG OF ROSEMARY
1 SPRIG OF SAGE
1 HANDFUL OF ITALIAN PARSLEY
15ml (1 Tbs) OREGANO
125ml (1/2 cup) OLIVE OIL
700ml (2 3/4 cups) BOTTLE TOMATO PASSATA (SIEVED TOMATO PUREE)*
5ml (1 tsp) SUGAR
125ml (1/2 cup) CREAM
SALT & PEPPER

Finely chop the garlic and the onion, and sauté them in the olive oil until golden.

Add the chopped herbs and cook for a few minutes over a medium heat, stirring gently with a wooden spoon. Add the tomato passata and simmer for approximately 15 minutes uncovered. Season to taste with salt, pepper and sugar. Stir in the cream (if desired).

Boil penne until "al dente", drain and stir into the sauce in the pot. Stir over medium heat until heated through.

NOTE: Pasta can be boiled ahead. Rinse with boiling water just before serving. Reheat the sauce and then toss in the pasta to heat through. Sauce can be made a few days ahead and either refrigerated or frozen.

* The kosher equivalent is to strain 3 x 400g (14 oz) cans whole peeled tomatoes and use that liquid to replace the Passata.

SERVES 6-8

POTATO GNOCCHI WITH ROASTED CHERRY TOMATOES AND SAGE

Once you have made and mastered these "light-as-a-feather" potato gnocchi you will never be able to eat any other!!!

1kg (2 lbs) BAKING POTATOES (3-4 LARGE POTATOES)
2 EGGS
PINCH OF SALT
250g (8 oz) FLOUR
10ml (2 tsps) BAKING POWDER

Boil the potatoes with the skin on, then peel them and put them through a potato ricer or mash them very finely and leave to cool.

Add flour, salt, egg and baking powder. Knead together very quickly to make dough.

Bring a large pot of water to a boil with lots of salt. Take small balls of dough and roll into finger-shaped cylinders, about 30cm (2 inches) long. Cut them into 2cm (0.8 inch) pieces with a sharp knife. Scrape with a fork to make a pattern on them so that they look like an oval. Drop a few at a time into the boiling water and let them to rise to the surface. Boil for 2 minutes, moving them around in the water. When puffed, immediately remove with a slotted spoon, place in one flat layer in an open casserole and drizzle with a little olive oil.

SWEET PEAS, ROASTED CHERRY TOMATOES AND SAGE
500g (1 lb) FROZEN PETIT POIS, DEFROSTED
400g (14 oz) ROSA CHERRY TOMATOES
30ml (2 Tbs) CHOPPED PARSLEY
RIND OF 1 LEMON
125g (4 oz) SAGE, BROKEN
80ml (1/3 cup) OLIVE OIL

Heat olive oil in a large frying pan. Add cherry tomatoes and season very well. Sauté until just about to burst. Remove with a slotted spoon onto a small plate. Place sage in the same oil and fry quickly so that it crisps. Remove and set aside. Place tomatoes back in pan. Add peas, parsley, lemon rind and heat through. Adjust seasoning. Pour sauce over gnocchi. Sprinkle with fried sage leaves. Preheat oven to 180°C (375°F). Place uncovered in oven and bake for 15 minutes.

NOTE: This makes one or two large dishes of gnocchi. The gnocchi can be made ahead and refrigerated, but only make the sauce on the day of serving.

SERVES 10

MIXED SQUASH GNOCCHI WITH SAGE OIL

These gnocchi are light and delicious and the sage oil with which they are topped enhances their flavour. They can be made ahead and baked before eating.

250g (8 oz) FLESH OF 2 GEM SQUASH
250g (8 oz) HUBBARD SQUASH, COOKED
250g (8 oz) BUTTERNUT, COOKED

2 JUMBO EGGS, BEATEN
15ml (2 Tbs) SALTED BUTTER or MARGARINE, MELTED
375ml (1 1/2 cups) FLOUR

SALT AND PEPPER

Mix all squashes together, ensuring that they are very well drained and quite dry or the gnocchi mixture will be very moist and you will have to add extra flour.

Beat the eggs. Add the butter and then the squash. Slowly add the flour and stir with a wooden spoon until just mixed in. Do not over mix.
Season with salt and pepper. Set aside.

Bring a large pot of very salty water to a boil. Drop dessertspoonfuls of mixture into the water, a few at a time. When they float to the top they are ready (this takes 2 minutes). Remove with a slotted spoon.

Place them in one flat layer in an open sprayed baking dish. Continue until all the mixture is cooked. Set aside to cool. Drizzle with the sage oil.

SAGE OIL
250ml (1 cup) SAGE LEAVES
125ml (1/2 cup) OLIVE OIL
SALT AND PEPPER

Blanch sage for 1 minute in a pot of boiling water. Remove, drain and rinse with cold water.

Place in a food processor with the oil, salt and pepper. Process until it is as smooth as possible. Drizzle over the gnocchi.

Preheat oven to 200°C (400°F). Place gnocchi in the oven uncovered for 20-30 mins or until bubbling.

SERVES 8

MIXED SQUASH GNOCCHI WITH SAGE OIL

POTATO GNOCCHI WITH ROASTED CHERRY TOMATOES AND SAGE

FUSILLI WITH ASPARAGUS CREAM SAUCE

My favourite sauce because it is so easy to make, so glorious in colour and so delicious!

250g (8 oz) FUSILLI

375ml (1 $^{1}/_{2}$ cups) CREAM
400g (14 oz) FRESH GREEN ASPARAGUS
10ml (2 tsps) HERBAMARE or COARSE SALT
FRESHLY GROUND BLACK PEPPER

Heat cream until almost boiling. Cut up 300g (9 oz) asparagus into pieces. Simmer gently in the cream for about 6 minutes or until softened and cooked.

Place mixture in a food processor and process until smooth. Add herbamare and pepper. Adjust seasoning. Cut up remaining asparagus into very small pieces.

Boil pasta until "al dente" in very salty water. Drain.

Place sauce back in the pot and simmer to cook remaining asparagus pieces. Stir in cooked pasta. Serve immediately.

NOTE: This sauce can be made ahead and reheated. If reheating, cool sauce before adding the additional asparagus cuts.

SERVES 4

LEMON AND ASPARAGUS PENNE

This is a delicious fresh looking and tasting pasta. The vibrant colours of the asparagus and peas contrast with the lemon-flavoured penne.

250g (8 oz) PENNE

500g (16 oz) ASPARAGUS, GRILLED
125ml ($^{1}/_{2}$ cup) FROZEN PETIT POIS
75g (2$^{1}/_{2}$ oz) SNOW PEAS, GRILLED (GRILL WITH ASPARAGUS)
60ml ($^{1}/_{4}$ cup) OLIVE OIL
2.5ml ($^{1}/_{2}$ tsp) CHILLI PASTE (OPTIONAL)
RIND OF 1 LEMON
JUICE OF 1 LEMON
175ml ($^{3}/_{4}$ cup) CRUMBLED FETA or PARMESAN CHEESE (OPTIONAL)
COARSE SALT AND BLACK PEPPER

Grill asparagus and snow peas whole, drizzled with a little olive oil, salt and pepper on a foil-lined baking tray directly under the grill for 5 minutes, turning once. After grilling, cut asparagus into 3, and snow peas in half.

Heat olive oil and chilli paste in a small pot. Add lemon rind, lemon juice and frozen peas, and simmer just until heated through. Do not overcook or peas will change colour.

Boil pasta until "al dente" and drain.

Toss the warm sauce over hot pasta, adding grilled asparagus and peas. Season with lots of salt and pepper, adding a little grated feta or parmesan for taste.

SERVES 4

SPICY SPAGHETTI ALLA PUTTANESCA

If you like a little spice in your life, this sauce combines many wonderful, spicy flavours.

375g (12 oz) SPAGHETTI

45ml (3 Tbs) OLIVE OIL
5ml (1 tsp) MINCED GARLIC
2 RED CHILLIES, CHOPPED
6 ANCHOVIES, CHOPPED
2 x 400g (14 oz) CANS WHOLE PEELED TOMATOES, CHOPPED
200g (7 oz) BLACK OLIVES HALVED, PITTED AND CHOPPED
SALT AND BLACK PEPPER

In a large pot, heat the oil and then add the garlic, chilli and anchovies and sauté for 1 minute. Stir in the tomatoes and olives. Bring to a boil, turn down stove and simmer for about 20 minutes until thickened.

Boil pasta in salted water until "al dente", drain and toss with sauce. Serve immediately.

NOTE: Sauce can be made ahead and refrigerated. Omit the chilli if you're not the spicy type!

SERVES 4

FUSILLI WITH ASPARAGUS CREAM SAUCE

LEMON AND ASPARAGUS PENNE

ROASTED BUTTERNUT AND ROSEMARY LASAGNE

A lasagne that is lighter than usual because it has thinner layers of vegetables and sauce. The butternut is sweet tasting and colourful, diced and baked that way.

12-16 FRESH LASAGNE SHEETS (HOMEMADE PASTA) or 12-16 READY-TO-USE LASAGNE SHEETS, BOILED IN A POT OF WATER TO SOFTEN THEM*

1kg (2.2 lbs) BUTTERNUT, CUT INTO SMALL DICE
45ml (3 Tbs) OLIVE OIL
SALT AND PEPPER

60ml (4 Tbs) BUTTER
10ml (2 tsps) MINCED GARLIC or 1 CLOVE GARLIC
60ml (1/4 cup) FLOUR
1 litre (4 cups) MILK
30ml (2 Tbs) FRESHLY CHOPPED ROSEMARY
15ml (1 Tbs) FRESHLY CHOPPED SAGE
1/2 ml (1/2 tsp) GROUND NUTMEG
SALT & PEPPER

Preheat oven to 220°C (440°F).

Place half of butternut in a single layer in a roasting pan. Drizzle with a little olive oil and season with salt and pepper. Roast on bottom rack of oven until golden - about 10-15 mins. Set that butternut aside and repeat procedure with remaining butternut. Set aside until ready to use.

In a large pot, melt the butter and then add the garlic and sauté until softened. Then stir in the flour and cook for 1 min. Slowly whisk in the milk until heated through and thickened. Then add rosemary and sage. Season to taste with salt, pepper and nutmeg.

Turn oven down to 180°C (375°F). Spray a medium-size ovenproof dish with non-stick cooking spray.

Spoon 1/3 of sauce on bottom of dish. Top with some lasagne sheets. Dot half of butternut over lasagne. Top with more sauce. Then more lasagne, then more butternut, lasagne and finally ending with sauce.

The top sheets of lasagne must be covered generously with sauce or they will dry out. Allow to rest for at least 1-2 hours before baking to soften the sheets.

Bake on middle rack of oven covered with foil for first 1/2 hour of cooking. Remove foil and continue baking for another 40-50 minutes or until lasagne sheets are soft.

NOTE: Can be prepared and refrigerated a day ahead. Do not freeze. It is best baked, however, when eaten immediately or it will dry out.

* Fresh lasagne sheets will cook much faster than the store-bought ones, as they are thinner. Do not overlap them, and they must be used raw (uncooked).

Ready-to-use lasagne sheets are thick and need to be boiled quickly for a few minutes before using. Drain them on dish cloths whilst preparing the sauce.

These must also not be overlapped. When using the bought lasagne sheets ensure that the lasagne stands for a few hours before cooking to soften it.

SERVES 6-8

FARFALLE WITH SPINACH

You will love this bright contrast of colour, texture and flavour. The crunchy pine nuts complete this dish.

250g (8 oz) FARFALLE, COOKED

15ml (1 Tbs) BUTTER
80ml (1/3 cup) OLIVE OIL
80ml (1/3 cup) PINE NUTS
10ml (2 tsps) MINCED GARLIC
150g (5 oz) FRESH SPINACH, VERY FINELY SHREDDED
4 LARGE TOMATOES, SEEDED AND CHOPPED
100g (3 oz) FETA CHEESE, CRUMBLED
150g (5 oz) PARMESAN CHEESE, GRATED
(or extra feta)
SALT & PEPPER

Melt the butter and 30ml (2 Tbs) of the olive oil in a large pan. Add pine nuts and garlic and sauté until golden. Then add spinach, tomatoes and seasoning. Sauté quickly until just heated through.

Boil pasta until "al dente".

Toss pasta with remaining oil. Add to sauce in frying pan. Stir in cheeses, taste for seasoning and toss very well. Serve immediately.

SERVES 4

RIGATONI WITH ZUCCHINI SAUCE & GREMOLATA

FARFALLE WITH SPINACH

RIGATONI WITH ZUCCHINI SAUCE AND GREMOLATA

This pasta sauce is creamy but not too rich and makes an excellent vegetarian accompaniment to any fish dish.

250g (8 oz) RIGATONI or PENNE
250g (8 oz) ZUCCHINI, GRATED
45ml (3 Tbs) BUTTER
45ml (3 Tbs) FLOUR
625ml (2½ cups) MILK
17.5ml (1½ Tbs) MAGGI VEGETABLE STOCK POWDER or
30ml (2 Tbs) TELMA PAREVE CHICKEN STOCK POWDER
SALT & PEPPER

Grate zucchini and place in a strainer. Salt generously to drain excess liquid for approx. 20 mins. Then rinse very well and pat dry. Set aside.

In a large frying pan, melt the butter. Stir in the flour and cook for 1 minute. Whisk in the milk and stock powder until thickened. Adjust seasoning. When thickened, add the grated zucchini.

Boil pasta until "al dente". Stir into sauce just before serving.

GREMOLATA
125ml (½ cup) ITALIAN BREAD CRUMBS
2.5ml (½ tsp) MINCED GARLIC or 1 GARLIC CLOVE (OPTIONAL)
30ml (2 Tbs) OLIVE OIL
30ml (2 Tbs) CHOPPED PARSLEY

Preheat oven to 140°C (325°F).

Dry out an Italian ciabatta in the oven and process in food processor until bread resembles coarse crumbs. Place crumbs in a frying pan with the olive oil and heat, gently stirring until browned. Remove from stove, add garlic and parsley and season with a little salt. Sprinkle over top of pasta just before serving.

NOTE: Pasta and sauce can be placed in a dish and refrigerated the day before serving. Heat either in a low oven 160°C (350°F) or in the microwave on high for a few minutes. Do not sprinkle with gremolata until after heated.

SERVES 6

LOW FAT SPINACH AND VEGETABLE LASAGNE

A delicious, low fat, two-minute lasagne without a white sauce. It must be baked covered first, or the lasagne sheets will be dry. Uncover to brown, and enjoy.

1 SMALL EGGPLANT, CUBED WITH SKIN
200g (7 oz) BABY SPINACH, COARSELY SHREDDED
45ml (3 Tbs) OLIVE OIL
2 x 400g (14 oz) CANS ALL GOLD ITALIAN STYLE SLICED TOMATOES
5ml (1 tsp) SALT
5ml (1 tsp) SUGAR
BLACK PEPPER
500g (2 cups) CHUNKY COTTAGE CHEESE
30ml (2 Tbs) CHOPPED PARSLEY
SALT, PEPPER TO TASTE
375ml (1½ cups) GRATED FETA or PARMESAN CHEESE
½ BOX READY-TO-USE LASAGNE SHEETS (I like the green ones)

Preheat oven to 180°C (375°F). Spray a deep, small ovenproof dish.
Fry eggplant in a pan with olive oil until softened, seasoning whilst frying. Set aside. In the same pan, wilt the spinach and season with salt and pepper. Set aside with eggplant. In a food processor, combine canned tomatoes, salt and sugar and pulse until coarsely chopped. Season with black pepper. Set aside. In the same bowl, process cottage cheese until smooth. Add ⅓ of feta or parmesan, parsley, salt and pepper to taste. Remove from bowl and stir in spinach and eggplant.

Spread ⅓ tomato mixture on bottom of dish. Cover with 3 lasagne sheets next to each other. Spread with ½ cottage cheese mixture. Cover with another 3 sheets next to each other. Spoon on another ⅓ tomato mixture and sprinkle with another ⅓ of parmesan or feta. Continue with more lasagne. Spread remaining cottage cheese mixture. Top with 3 more sheets and end with remaining tomato mixture. Cover with foil. Allow to stand for about 1 hour before baking to soften the lasagne sheets.

Bake 40 mins covered. Remove foil and sprinkle with remaining feta or parmesan. Bake uncovered for a further 20-25 mins. or until noodles are soft and cheese has melted. Prick with a fork to test if lasagne is soft. Allow to rest for 20 minutes before serving.

Note: This is best when made ahead and refrigerated as the lasagne sheets soften and absorb the liquid. Do not overlap them, or they will take longer to bake. It can be frozen unbaked, but defrost before baking.

SERVES 8

LOW FAT SPINACH AND VEGETABLE LASAGNE

SPICY BEEF AND VEGETABLE STIR-FRY

Meat

OSSOBUCO

SWEET AND STICKY BEEF RIBS

BARBECUED BEEF KEBABS

ASIAN STYLE LAMB

Meat

Meat

It is always a favourite as long as the quality is good and it is well matured and not too fresh. The richer the colour, the more tender the meat. Vacuum packed meat becomes more tender with age and can be refrigerated for up to 10 days and then frozen.

Veal, lamb and beef are the most popular types and lend themselves to a variety of sauces and cuisine. Fresh herbs are essential and I despise using MSG in any spices as it gives an unnatural flavour.

It is important to only use salt and pepper just before the cooking process, and not during marinating as it toughens meat. I always use coarse salt and freshly ground black pepper. Salt crystals dissolve quicker in a sauce rather than rock salt, which tends to take a long time. Where possible, buy the wonderful grinders which are available.

Beef should preferably be served medium-rare, as it gets tougher the longer it is cooked, while lamb should be served more on the medium side and veal needs the shortest time of all unless you are roasting.

Enjoy these delicious and tasty sauces and marinades which accompany each dish.

Meat

QUICK AND EASY

- MEXICAN STEAK FAJITAS
- LAMB AND ROSEMARY KEBABS

RECIPES

- LAMB SHANK TAGINE WITH COUSCOUS
- ASIAN STYLE LAMB
- OSSOBUCO
- SWEET AND STICKY BEEF RIBS
- VEAL STIR-FRY WITH NOODLES
- BARBECUED BEEF KEBABS
- SPICY BEEF AND VEGETABLE STIR-FRY
- BEEF TOURNEDOS ON POLENTA CAKES WITH SALSA VERDE
- BRISKET WITH CARAMELISED ONIONS
- HERB-CRUSTED STANDING PRIME RIB ROAST
- RACK OF LAMB WITH MINT SYRUP
- GREEK LAMB KLEFTIKO

MEXICAN STEAK FAJITAS

Perfect for leftover roast, steak, chicken breasts or lamb. Just cut into thin strips and fill the tortilla or pita with guacamole and salsa.

10 FLOUR TORTILLAS* or PITAS

To prepare fajitas - preheat a frying pan and brown tortillas lightly on each side. Stack in a dish. Cover with plastic wrap and reheat for 1-2 minutes in the microwave before using. Serve warm.

1.5kg (3.3 lbs) LONDON BROIL or BOLO ROAST or
4 THICK RUMP STEAKS**

MARINADE
125ml (1/2 cup) TOMATO SAUCE
30ml (2 Tbs) SYRUP or HONEY
15ml (1 Tbs) WORCESTERSHIRE SAUCE
30ml (2 Tbs) DIJON MUSTARD or WHOLEGRAIN MUSTARD
45ml (3 Tbs) SOYA SAUCE
SALT AND PEPPER

Preheat a grilling pan or barbecue. Spray with olive oil spray.

Mix all marinade ingredients together. Pour over meat and marinate for a few hours before grilling. Season meat with salt and pepper. Then grill, basting with sauce continuously until medium rare. Cut into thin slices before serving.

SALSA
1 BOTTLE OLD EL PASO SALSA (medium)*** or
HOMEMADE SALSA:
4-6 TOMATOES, CHOPPED
1/2 RED ONION, CHOPPED
1 RED or GREEN CHILLI, CHOPPED FINELY
COARSE SALT AND PEPPER

Mix all ingredients together and set aside.

GUACAMOLE
3 LARGE AVOCADOES, CUT INTO LARGE CHUNKS
2 TOMATOES, CHOPPED
1/2 RED ONION, CHOPPED
JUICE OF 1 LEMON
COARSE SALT
CHILLI (AS DESIRED)

Mix all ingredients together leaving mixture quite chunky.

TO SERVE: Spread a little guacamole on the tortilla or pita. Top with some meat slices and salsa. Roll up and eat.

* Old El Paso Burrito Tortillas or homemade tortillas - see appendix

** London Broil and Bolo Roast are much thicker than rump steaks and will take about half an hour to grill. Ensure grill is not too hot, or the meat will burn on the outside, but not cook inside.

*** See Appendix.

SERVES 8-10

LAMB AND ROSEMARY KEBABS

6 THICK LAMB SHOULDER or RIB CHOPS
(ABOUT 2cm (1 inch) THICK)
5ml (1 tsp) DRY ROSEMARY
125ml (1/2 cup) CREAMY HERB SALAD DRESSING*
30ml (2 Tbs) OLIVE OIL
30ml (2 Tbs) LEMON JUICE
COARSE SALT
BLACK PEPPER

8-10 WHITE MUSHROOMS, BLANCHED**
8-10 BABY ONIONS, BLANCHED**
1 RED PEPPER, CUT INTO THICK SLICES

Cut lamb into thick cubes and thread onto kebab sticks alternating with mushrooms, baby onions and red pepper. Marinate in a mixture of rosemary, herb dressing, olive oil, lemon juice and seasoning.

Preheat grilling pan on medium heat. Spray with olive oil spray. Grill for about 10-15 minutes on each side, or until well browned, leaving the centre a little pink. Serve immediately.

* I use Ina Paarman Herb Salad dressing, but any creamy herb or other creamy dressing will be fine.

** Boil a small pot of water. Place mushrooms in water and boil for 1 minute, then drain. Onions need to boil for 5 minutes.

SERVES 8

WHOLEGRAIN MUSTARD

LAMB SHANK TAGINE WITH COUSCOUS

There is nothing nicer than tasty, soft meat that falls off the bone and is full of flavour. This dish conjures up all that. It is particularly delicious when made in advance.

5 KOSHER LAMB SHANKS or 10 NON-KOSHER SHANKS - BONE MUST BE BROKEN TWICE - ASK BUTCHER (The kosher ones are generally much larger than the non-kosher)
SALT & PEPPER

2 ONIONS, CHOPPED VERY COARSELY
6 LARGE CARROTS, CUT INTO CHUNKS
1 WHOLE BUTTERNUT, PEELED AND CUT INTO PIECES
10 BABY POTATOES WITH SKIN, CUT IN HALF VERTICALLY

10ml (2 tsps) GINGER
10ml (2 tsps) CORIANDER
10ml (2 tsps) CUMIN
10ml (2 tsps) CARDAMOM
125ml ($^1/_2$ cup) SOYA SAUCE
500ml (2 cups) BEEF STOCK
A FEW SPRIGS OF FRESH ROSEMARY
200ml ($^2/_3$ cup) SUN-DRIED TOMATO SAUCE**
125ml ($^1/_2$ cup) APRICOT JAM

Preheat oven to 160°C (350°F).

Season shanks with salt and pepper on all sides. Brown well in a large non-stick pot. Remove and set aside in an ovenproof casserole.

In the same pot, brown onions in a drop of olive oil. Place these on top of meat.

Heat the spices in the pot for a few minutes. Then whisk in the soya and beef stock. Pour sauce over meat. Scatter chunks of carrots and sprigs of rosemary around the casserole.

Roast in oven covered with foil or a lid for 2 hours, basting frequently.*

Uncover after 2 hours. Adjust seasoning. Add potatoes, sun-dried tomato sauce and butternut pieces. Bake uncovered for another 1$^1/_2$ hours. Then stir in the apricot jam for the last half hour.

COUSCOUS
Prepare as per instructions on container, except add stock to the water and a little turmeric or saffron. Steam for 5 minutes off the stove. Then fluff and add extra liquid (if necessary), a little chopped parsley and extra seasoning.
Serve with the meat.

NOTE: This dish reheats beautifully. The flavour permeates the meat even more if made a few days ahead. It can be made ahead and frozen without potatoes.

* NON-KOSHER - Roast 1 hour covered and 1$^1/_2$ hours uncovered (because the meat is smaller it will take less time to cook)
** I use Ina Paarman Coat and Cook Sun-dried tomato sauce.

SERVES 8-10

ASIAN STYLE LAMB

We love a very soft and tender lamb, and this one is particularly delicious with its orange-flavoured sauce.

2.5kg (5 lb) SHOULDER or 2kg (4$^1/_2$ lb) LEG OF LAMB

MARINADE
125ml ($^1/_2$ cup) SOYA SAUCE
45ml (3 Tbs) HONEY
125ml ($^1/_2$ cup) ORANGE JUICE
45ml (3 Tbs) OLIVE OIL
10ml (2 tsps) PAPRIKA
SALT & PEPPER

Mix all marinade ingredients together.
Place meat in a sprayed roasting pan. Pour marinade over the lamb 24 hours before cooking.

Preheat oven to 160°C (350°F). Cover meat with foil and roast on the middle rack of oven for 2 hours basting continuously. Uncover and roast for a further $^1/_2$ hour or until well browned.

NOTE: Meat can also be removed from oven after the first 2 hours then barbecued for 20 minutes.
It can be prepared in advance and reheated, as the sauce permeates the meat to give it even more taste.

SERVES 10

LAMB SHANK TAGINE WITH COUSCOUS

OSSOBUCO

A wonderful, tender and tasty veal dish made in the authentic Italian manner.

2kg ($4\frac{1}{2}$ lbs) VEAL SHANKS or BEEF SHANKS (CUT QUITE THICK)
125ml ($\frac{1}{2}$ cup) FLOUR
SALT AND PEPPER
30ml (2 Tbs) OLIVE OIL
1 ONION, CHOPPED
5ml (1 tsp) MINCED GARLIC or 1 LARGE CLOVE GARLIC, CHOPPED
250ml (1 cup) WHITE WINE
3 x 400g (14 oz) CANS WHOLE PEELED TOMATOES, FINELY CHOPPED AND STRAINED*
60ml (4 Tbs) ITALIAN PARSLEY, CHOPPED
3 SPRIGS ROSEMARY, STEM OFF
2 SPRIGS OREGANO, STEM OFF
JUICE OF $\frac{1}{2}$ LEMON
250ml (1 cup) CHICKEN STOCK (1 Tbs CHICKEN STOCK POWDER DISSOLVED IN WATER)
250ml (1 cup) COLD WATER

Preheat oven to 160°C (350°F).

Season flour very well with salt and pepper. Heat 1 Tbs of olive oil in a frying pan and dip shanks into the seasoned flour. Sear on both sides until all the meat has been browned. Place in an ovenproof casserole dish.

Chop onion and garlic and fry until golden in remaining olive oil. Add the white wine and let it evaporate. Add drained tomatoes, stock and water. Bring to a boil.

Add parsley, rosemary, oregano and lemon juice. Season to taste with salt and pepper. Pour over the meat and cover dish with a lid or foil.

Bake on middle rack of oven for at least 2 hours or until the meat is softened. Remove foil and sauce will have thickened. Adjust seasoning, adding a pinch of sugar if necessary.

NOTE: This dish may be frozen, defrosted and reheated in a medium oven for about 20-25 mins, or may be made a few days in advance and refrigerated.

* 700ml ($2\frac{2}{3}$ cups) Bottle of Italian Passata may be substituted for the 3 cans tomatoes. These are available in most supermarkets, and have already been chopped and strained.

SERVES 8

SWEET AND STICKY BEEF RIBS

Your guests will be licking their lips and begging for more when they taste these delicious ribs. They are definitely worth making!

7 SLABS OF SHORT BEEF RIBS (CUT SHORT - ABOUT 7.5cms (3 inches) THICK)

MARINADE
250ml (1 cup) TOMATO SAUCE
385g ($9\frac{1}{2}$ oz) CAN CRUSHED PINEAPPLE
5ml (1 tsp) GARLIC SALT
5ml (1 tsp) ONION SALT
5ml (1 tsp) PAPRIKA
45ml (3 Tbs) WORCESTERSHIRE SAUCE
80ml ($\frac{1}{3}$ cup) SOYA SAUCE
125ml ($\frac{1}{2}$ cup) ANY MEAT MARINADE
250ml (1 cup) WATER
250ml (1 cup) FRUIT CHUTNEY

Place uncooked beef ribs in cold water in a large pot. Bring to a boil, reduce heat and simmer for at least 45 minutes. Drain and allow ribs to cool.

In the meantime, mix all ingredients for marinade together. Place cooked ribs in a roasting pan and cover with the marinade. Allow to marinate for at least 24 hours before cooking.

Preheat oven to 180°C (375°F).

Place ribs in oven covered and roast for about 1 hour. Uncover and brown for a further $\frac{1}{2}$ hour.

NOTE: You might need to add extra water if sauce gets too thick.

SERVES 8

SWEET AND STICKY BEEF RIBS

VEAL STIR-FRY WITH VEGETABLES

The veal is very tender when stir-fried and tastes marvellous with the addition of the vegetables. Serve on a bed of noodles or with steamed Jasmine rice.

1kg (2.2 lbs) VEAL or BEEF STRIPS
30ml (2 Tbs) OLIVE OIL
SALT AND PEPPER

Toss cut veal or beef strips with olive oil, salt and pepper. Set aside.

SAUCE
60ml (1/4 cup) APRICOT JAM
90ml (6 Tbs) SOYA SAUCE
30ml (2 Tbs) TOMATO SAUCE
125ml (1/2 cup) WATER

Stir all sauce ingredients together. Set aside.

250g (8 oz) MUSHROOMS, CUT IN HALF
1 CARROT, JULIENNED
1/2 RED PEPPER, CUT INTO STRIPS
1/2 YELLOW PEPPER, CUT INTO STRIPS
500ml (2 cups) BEAN SPROUTS
1 BOK CHOY, CHOPPED COARSELY

Heat wok until very hot. Add the meat in batches and stir-fry very quickly to sear meat, but not cook completely. Set aside in a bowl.

Stir-fry mushrooms and carrot, seasoning well until mushrooms are dry. Then add peppers, bean sprouts and bok choy and stir-fry very quickly until almost cooked. Set aside with meat.

Pour sauce into the wok and boil rapidly until reduced and thickened. Place everything back in the wok and toss quickly to coat the meat and vegetables. Serve immediately.

SERVES 4-6

BARBECUED BEEF KEBABS

Grilled kebabs with a wonderful, authentic BBQ sauce.

12 BEEF KEBABS (USING SIDE BOLO ROAST or RUMP STEAK), WITH 6 CUBES ON EACH WOODEN or METAL SKEWERS

MARINADE
45ml (3 Tbs) TREACLE BROWN SUGAR
500ml (2 cups) TOMATO SAUCE
125ml (1/2 cup) MOLASSES
60ml (1/4 cup) WHOLEGRAIN MUSTARD
30ml (2 Tbs) WORCESTERSHIRE SAUCE
10ml (2 tsps) PAPRIKA
5ml (1 tsp) GARLIC SALT
5ml (1 tsp) ONION SALT

Whisk all ingredients together.

At least 24 hours before serving, place kebabs in a shallow roasting pan and brush well with the marinade, coating all sides.

Preheat grill in oven. Grill kebabs for 5 minutes on each side directly under the grill. Meat should be medium-rare in the middle and very tender.

Serve immediately.

NOTE: Vegetables can be alternated with the meat on the kebab sticks, if desired.

SERVES 10-12

VEAL STIR-FRY AND VEGETABLES

SPICY BEEF AND VEGETABLE STIR-FRY

I love making a stir-fry because it is so quick and easy, and I usually use whatever vegetables I have in the fridge. These make a delicious, slightly spicy dish.

500g (1 lb) SCOTCH FILLET or RUMP STEAK

MARINADE
175ml (3/4 cup) CHICKEN STOCK (1 TELMA or 1/2 KNORR CUBE)
60ml (1/4 cup) HOISIN SAUCE* or MEAT MARINADE
30ml (2 Tbs) SWEET CHILLI SAUCE*
15ml (1 Tbs) SOYA SAUCE
15ml (1 Tbs) SESAME OIL*

Cut meat into thin strips and marinate in above ingredients for half an hour. Set aside.

45ml (3 Tbs) OLIVE OIL
1 ONION, THINLY SLICED
10ml (2 tsps) MINCED GARLIC or 2 CLOVES GARLIC, CRUSHED
250g (4 oz) SMALL MUSHROOMS, WHOLE
1 CARROT, CUT INTO VERY THIN SLICES
500g (1 lb) SWEET POTATOES, CUT INTO THIN JULIENNE
4 SPRING ONIONS, CUT ON DIAGONAL
250g (8 oz) SNOW PEAS

Heat olive oil in wok until almost smoking. Quickly stir-fry onion and garlic until golden. Then add mushrooms and fry until most of the liquid has evaporated. Add carrot, sweet potato and spring onion. Stir-fry on high for 2 minutes, seasoning well. Set aside.

Drain meat from marinade and quickly stir-fry in batches until almost cooked, browned and sealed. Set aside on a separate plate. When all meat has been seared, place marinade back into wok and boil until slightly reduced.

Return vegetables and meat back into wok. Add snow peas and quickly stir-fry to complete cooking the meat and heating the vegetables.

Serve immediately.

* See appendix

SERVES 4

BEEF TOURNEDOS ON POLENTA CAKES WITH SALSA VERDE

What an elegant main course this makes. It looks beautiful and tastes equally delectable.

1kg (2.2 lbs) BEEF SCOTCH FILLET or FILLET, CUT INTO STEAKS 3cm (1 inch) THICK

SAUCE
500ml (2 cups) BEEF STOCK (4 tsps BEEF STOCK POWDER)
500ml (2 cups) SWEET WINE or SHERRY
5ml (1 tsp) MAIZENA (CORNSTARCH) DISSOLVED IN A LITTLE COLD WATER

Preheat oven to 220°C (440°F).
Season meat well with salt and pepper. Heat a heavy-bottomed grilling pan until very hot. Sear steaks 3 mins each side. Place on a baking tray and roast for a further 5-8 minutes.

In the same pan, add sherry and beef stock and reduce on high heat for 5 minutes. Whisk in a little maizena to thicken. Set aside and reheat when ready to use.

POLENTA
625ml (2 1/2 cups) BOILING WATER
5ml (1 tsp) SALT
250ml (1 cup) POLENTA
15ml (1 Tbs) MARGARINE

Bring water and salt to a boil. Whisk in polenta and stir until thickened for approximately 5 minutes. Add margarine and continue stirring until mixture pulls away from the sides of the pot. Spread on to a board. Allow to cool and then cut into thick rounds.

Preheat oven to 180°C (375°F). Place rounds on a sprayed baking tray, brush with a little olive oil and bake for 10 minutes or until golden, turning over once. These should be baked just before serving.

SALSA VERDE
5ml (1 tsp) MINCED GARLIC
10ml (2 tsps) CHOPPED PARSLEY
10ml (2 tsps) WHOLEGRAIN MUSTARD
30ml (2 Tbs) APPLE CIDER VINEGAR
125ml (1/2 cup) OLIVE OIL

Stir all ingredients together and set aside until ready to use.

TO SERVE: Place polenta cake on bottom of plate. Top with tournedos and spoon sauce over meat and around plate.

SERVES 4

BEEF TOURNEDOS ON POLENTA CAKES WITH SALSA VERDE

BRISKET WITH CARAMELISED ONIONS

Brisket is one of those tough meats that require a long cooking time for the meat to soften. This one has a superb flavour and it is even tastier when made in advance.

2kg (4½ lb) FRESH BRISKET
3 ONIONS, SLICED
15ml (1 Tbs) OLIVE OIL
45ml (3 Tbs) SUGAR
250g (8 oz) MUSHROOMS, WHOLE
200g (7 oz) BABY CARROTS, PEELED
6 ITALIAN ROMA TOMATOES

500ml (2 cups) BEEF STOCK (1 TELMA or 1 KNORR BEEF STOCK CUBES)
250ml (1 cup) KOSHER SWEET WINE or PORT
60ml (¼ cup) BALSAMIC VINEGAR
60ml (¼ cup) TOMATO SAUCE

Preheat oven to 160°C (350°F).

Sauté onions in a large frying pan in the olive oil on medium heat until softened and golden for about 15 minutes. Add sugar just before removing from stove. Set aside.

Season meat on all sides. Turn stove to high and brown the roast on both sides in the same frying pan. Pour over 1 cup of the beef stock and place in a roasting pan.

Sauté mushrooms and carrots in same frying pan for a few minutes. Place around the roast. Slice the tomatoes and sauté in the same pan until just softened and then place on top of roast.

Boil Kosher Sweet Wine or Port, remaining cup of beef stock, balsamic vinegar and tomato sauce on high until bubbling and slightly reduced. Set aside. Cover meat and vegetables with foil and roast on middle rack of oven for 2 hours.

Uncover after 2 hours, pour over reduced sauce and continue roasting brisket for another 1 hour uncovered. Cool and then slice. Layer into a serving dish, spooning over the sauce, and then placing caramelised onions down the top of the roast.

NOTE: Can be refrigerated a few days before. Freezes very well. Defrost and reheat on 140°C (325°F) covered for 40-45 minutes or until heated through.

SERVES 10-12

HERB-CRUSTED STANDING PRIME RIB ROAST

An outstanding roast flavoured with fresh herbs and surrounded by mushrooms and potatoes.

2.5kg (5½ lbs) PRIME RIB ROAST, SCOTCH FILLET or RUMP ROAST
SALT AND PEPPER

MARINADE
250ml (1 cup) OIL-FREE ITALIAN SALAD DRESSING
10ml (2 tsps) MINCED GARLIC
80ml (⅓ cup) FRESH SAGE, CHOPPED
80ml (⅓ cup) FRESH OREGANO, CHOPPED
60ml (¼ cup) FRESH THYME, CHOPPED
60ml (¼ cup) OLIVE OIL
COARSE SALT
BLACK PEPPER

4 POTATOES, CUBED
500g (1 lb) MUSHROOMS, WHOLE

Season roast very well. Coat with salad dressing, olive oil and fresh herbs and marinate overnight in a sprayed roasting pan.

Preheat oven to 200°C (400°F).

Remove roast from roasting pan and set aside on a plate, covered with foil while you roast the vegetables. Place potatoes and mushrooms in the same roasting pan and season well with salt and pepper, allowing them to roast until golden for about 30 minutes. Remove and set aside.

Place the meat back into the roasting pan and roast for 1 hour uncovered.

Season roast again, add vegetables and for a further 30 minutes with the vegetables. Baste the meat with any gravy from the bottom of the pan.

Cover roasting pan with foil and rest meat for 10 minutes before carving.

NOTE: This roast should be served medium-rare for the meat to be soft and tender.

SERVES 10-12

BRISKET WITH CARAMELISED ONIONS

HERB-CRUSTED STANDING PRIME RIB ROAST

RACK OF LAMB WITH MINT SYRUP

I have yet to meet anyone who does not love rack of lamb. This one is special because the mint complements the lamb to perfection.

4 WHOLE RACKS OF LAMB (with approx. 8-9 chops each), TRIMMED OF ALL FAT AND WITH THE TOP BONE EXPOSED

30g (1 oz) CHIVES, CUT INTO PIECES
330ml (1 1/3 cup) WHITE WINE
250ml (1 cup) MINT JELLY or SAUCE
2.5ml (1/2 tsp) CHILLI PASTE or POWDER (OPTIONAL)
30ml (2 Tbs) FRESH ROSEMARY, CHOPPED
COARSE SALT
PEPPER

Place all sauce ingredients in food processor and process until almost smooth. Set aside until ready to use.

Preheat grill in the oven.
Place lamb in a roasting pan and pour over marinade. Marinate for at least 1/2 an hour before grilling.

Season racks very well. Place under grill for approx. 10 minutes in middle of oven and watch carefully to ensure they do not burn. Turn over when nicely browned and grill other side for a further 10 minutes.

If not cooked completely, turn oven down to 220°C (440°F) and roast for a further 15 minutes maximum.

Serve immediately.

NOTE: Rack of lamb, unlike other lamb should be served just medium, for the meat to be tender. Well-done racks are tough to eat.

SERVES 8-10 (Allow 3-4 chops per person)

GREEK LAMB - KLEFTIKO

This method of cooking lamb brings out the best taste. It falls off the bone and is moist, tender and succulent.

2kg (4.4 lb) SHOULDER or LEG OF LAMB

125ml (1/2 cup) OLIVE OIL
JUICE OF 2 LEMONS
45ml (3 Tbs) FRESH OREGANO
SALT AND PEPPER
500ml (2 cups) BEEF STOCK (2 TELMA or 1 KNORR CUBE)
30 BABY POTATOES

Marinate lamb in olive oil, lemon juice and oregano 24 hours in advance.

Preheat oven to 140°C (300°F). Place lamb in a roasting pan and cover well with foil. Roast covered for 3 hours, basting occasionally, and turning after each hour. Place whole baby potatoes around the meat after the first 2 hours.

After 3 hours pour the beef stock into the roasting pan. Uncover and allow meat to brown, turning to brown both sides and basting with the gravy.

Carve meat thinly and pour sauce over. Surround with the potatoes.

NOTE: This lamb is even better when it has been prepared a few days in advance as the flavour of the sauce permeates the meat. It freezes beautifully and can be reheated covered on 140°C (325°F) for about 45 minutes.

SERVES 10

RACK OF LAMB WITH MINT SYRUP

WHOLE ROAST CHICKEN WITH HERBS

Poultry

TANDOORI CHICKEN

POLLO ALLA TOSCANA

CHICKEN AND VEGETABLE RISOTTO

SESAME NOODLE CHICKEN STIR-FRY

Poultry

Poult

For many of you who love and enjoy chicken both at home or when eating out, you will appreciate this section.

You will love the wonderful sauces, combinations and cuts of chicken in these recipes, because there is something for everybody.

Chicken is low fat and healthy (without the skin) and has become both a staple and favourite in everybody's diet. It is versatile and with the addition of sauces, herbs and flavourings can be grilled, stir-fried, roasted, stewed or baked. Truly remarkable fare.

Unfortunately the chicken breast is the one part of the bird that cannot be prepared ahead as it dries out. It should be prepared just before eating for it to be succulent, juicy and above all "not dry". In order to give a breast colour for such a short cooking time, roasting on very high heat and grilling or pan-frying is essential. The perfect skinless and boneless chicken breast takes exactly 20 minutes to cook. A breast with skin and bone takes 30 minutes, chicken pieces 45 minutes and a whole chicken exactly 90 minutes. Cooked this way you will always produce golden brown and very moist pieces of chicken. High heat and grilling bring out the best flavour and colour. A variety of vegetables and interesting sauces transform any bird into a myriad of different meals.

QUICK AND EASY

- SWEET & SPICY CHICKEN BREASTS
- APRICOT, LIME AND SOYA CHICKEN
- CRUMBED BREASTS WITH CUCUMBER SALSA
- GRILLED CHICKEN KEBABS

RECIPES

- LEMON AND ROSEMARY CHICKEN WITH POTATOES
- WHOLE ROAST CHICKEN WITH HERBS
- POLLO ALLA TOSCANA
- CHICKEN AND PASTA BAKE
- SWEET CHILLI CHINESE CHICKEN WITH NOODLES
- CHICKEN AND VEGETABLE RISOTTO
- SESAME NOODLE AND CHICKEN STIR-FRY
- TANDOORI CHICKEN
- CASHEW CHICKEN WITH OYSTER MUSHROOMS
- TURKEY WITH ROASTED APPLE SAUCE
- COQ AU VIN

Poultry

SWEET & SPICY CHICKEN BREASTS

6 BONELESS CHICKEN BREASTS or
400g (14 oz) MINI CHICKEN BREAST FILLETS
125ml ($^1/_2$ cup) SMOOTH APRICOT JAM
30ml (2 Tbs) SOYA SAUCE
30ml (2 Tbs) APPLE CIDER VINEGAR or RICE VINEGAR
60ml ($^1/_4$ cup) BOILING WATER
5ml (1 tsp) CHILLI PASTE
SALT AND PEPPER

Season breasts with salt and pepper. Heat a grilling pan or barbecue. Spray pan with olive oil spray. Grill breasts for about 8 mins on each side on medium-high until golden and almost cooked through. Watch that they don't burn. Set aside and cover with foil. Whisk sauce ingredients together and boil in a pot until thickened and reduced. Sauce should be quite syrupy. Quickly sauté breasts in sauce coating all sides to complete the cooking process. Serve with steamed Jasmine or Basmati rice.

SERVES 4-6

APRICOT, LIME AND SOYA CHICKEN

1.5kg (3 lbs) CHICKEN PIECES
250ml (1 cup) SMOOTH APRICOT JAM
60ml ($^1/_4$ cup) SOYA SAUCE
60ml ($^1/_4$ cup) FRESH LIME JUICE or BOTTLED LEMON JUICE
SALT AND PEPPER

Mix all ingredients together in a bowl. Preheat oven to 180°C (375°F). Pour sauce over chicken pieces and roast for 25 minutes each side or until golden. Grill to brown just before serving.

SERVES 6

CRUMBED BREASTS WITH CUCUMBER SALSA

6 BONELESS AND SKINLESS BREASTS, LIGHTLY POUNDED

1 EGG BEATEN WITH 30ml (2 Tbs) COLD WATER
250ml (1 cup) KELLOGGS CORNFLAKE CRUMBS
10ml (2 tsps) THYME
10ml (2 tsps) ROSEMARY
5ml (1 tsp) ONION SALT
5ml (1 tsp) HERBAMARE
FRESHLY GROUND BLACK PEPPER

Preheat oven to 200°C (400°F).

Place a baking rack onto a foil-lined baking tray and spray rack with olive oil spray. Mix crumbs, herbs and seasonings in a bowl.

Dip chicken breasts into egg and then crumb mixture. If you have time, refrigerate for a few mins. or, place them on the baking rack and spray with a little olive oil spray.

Bake for 15-18 mins. Breasts should be completely cooked. Serve with the salsa.

CUCUMBER SALSA
$^1/_2$ ENGLISH CUCUMBER, PEELED, SEEDED AND GRATED
2 TOMATOES, PEELED, SEEDED AND CHOPPED
1 AVOCADO, DICED
30ml (2 Tbs) FRESH LEMON JUICE
15ml (1 Tbs) CHOPPED PARSLEY
SALT AND PEPPER
Mix all ingredients together.

SERVES 4

GRILLED CHICKEN KEBABS

METAL or WOODEN SKEWERS
80ml ($^1/_3$ cup) FRESHLY CHOPPED ROSEMARY

6 SKINLESS AND BONELESS CHICKEN BREASTS, or
10 BONELESS AND SKINLESS CHICKEN THIGHS
250g (8 oz) ROSA CHERRY TOMATOES
250g (8 oz) WHITE MUSHROOMS
1 RED ONION, CUT INTO WEDGES

SAUCE
375ml (1$^1/_2$ cups) INA PAARMAN COAT AND COOK SUN-DRIED TOMATO SAUCE
30ml (2 Tbs) WORCESTER SAUCE
30ml (2 Tbs) SOYA SAUCE
30ml (2 Tbs) HONEY
8-10 POUYOUKAS MILD PEPPADEWS*
SALT & PEPPER

Place all sauce ingredients in food processor and process until smooth.

Cut chicken into even-sized cubes. Thread on to skewers alternating with tomatoes, mushrooms and red onion. Use about 4 chicken cubes per skewer.

Place skewers on a flat baking tray, drizzle with sauce and sprinkle with rosemary. Season with additional salt and pepper.

Grill for about 20 minutes on a preheated grilling pan sprayed with olive oil spray or on a barbecue. Turn all the time and baste with sauce.

* Available in most supermarkets country wide and add a little spice to the sauce. If unavailable, use a little chilli paste or powder.

SERVES 6

CHICKEN AND PASTA BAKE

LEMON AND ROSEMARY CHICKEN WITH POTATOES

I love the simplicity of this dish. It is quite lemony, because the vegetables are flavoured by the chicken juices which drip on to them.

2 WHOLE CHICKENS, CUT INTO PIECES
30g (1 oz) FRESH ROSEMARY, CHOPPED
1kg (2.2 lbs) BABY POTATOES, CUT IN HALF WITH SKIN ON
6-8 LARGE CARROTS, CUT INTO CHUNKS or 200g (7 oz) BABY CARROTS, PEELED
JUICE OF 2-3 LEMONS
COARSE SALT AND BLACK PEPPER

Preheat oven to 200°C (400°F).
Place potatoes and carrots in a large roasting pan. Season well with salt, pepper and some rosemary. Spray a rack to fit over the roasting pan. Place chicken pieces on the rack above the vegetables and season well. Squeeze lemon juice over chicken and sprinkle with additional rosemary. Roast chicken & vegetables on bottom rack of oven for 25 minutes. Turn pieces over. Shake vegetables in bottom of roasting pan. Season both vegetables and chicken again. Bake for a further 25 minutes. Chicken should be golden. Turn on the grill for the last 5-10 minutes and grill chicken pieces to brown.

SERVES 6-8

WHOLE ROAST CHICKEN WITH HERBS

When I use fresh herbs on a chicken, they infuse and add a sensational flavour and aroma and make a beautiful brown, scrumptious roast.

1 WHOLE CHICKEN
45ml (3 Tbs) FRESH SAGE
45ml (3 Tbs) FRESH OREGANUM
45ml (3 Tbs) FRESH THYME
45ml (3 Tbs) FRESH ROSEMARY
60ml ($^1/_4$ cup) OLIVE OIL
COARSE SALT
HERBAMARE
FRESHLY GROUND BLACK PEPPER

Chop herbs, adding the olive oil and seasonings to make a paste. The mixture should be quite salty in order to give the chicken a delicious flavour. Spread some herb mixture under the skin of the chicken and some in the cavity of the chicken. Then spread some all over outside of chicken. Season again with salt, pepper and herbamare. Preheat oven to 200°C (400°F). Place chicken, breast side down in roasting pan and roast for 45 minutes. Turn over and roast on other side for 45 minutes.

NOTE: Chicken can be coated with the herbs the day before to marinate. After it is $^3/_4$ cooked it can be barbecued for the last 20 minutes to add to the flavour.

SERVES 4

POLLO ALLA TOSCANA

A truly Italian-inspired chicken dish bursting with a medley of wild mushrooms. Use whatever mushrooms are in season to add taste.

1 WHOLE CHICKEN CUT INTO PIECES or 1kg (2.2 lbs) CHICKEN PIECES

80ml ($^1/_3$ cup) OLIVE OIL
20g ($^1/_2$ oz) DRIED PORCINI MUSHROOMS*
250g (8 oz) PORTOBELLINI MUSHROOMS, HALVED
250g (8 oz) FRESH SHITAKE MUSHROOMS (IN SEASON) or WHITE MUSHROOMS
400g (14 oz) CAN ITALIAN WHOLE PEELED TOMATOES, CHOPPED
250ml (1 cup) WHITE WINE
SALT, PEPPER

* Soak in 175ml ($^3/_4$ cup) boiling water for 10 minutes or until softened

Preheat oven to 220°C (440°F).

Heat a large non-stick frying pan. Season chicken pieces well with salt and pepper and brown well on both sides. When all pieces are browned, remove and place in a roasting pan.

Add wine to the frying pan and reduce slightly. Add the porcini mushrooms including liquid, the tomatoes and the other mushrooms and bring to a boil. Season to taste and then pour everything over the chicken.

Roast uncovered for about 45-50 minutes. Grill to brown just before the end of cooking time.

NOTE: Can be made ahead and reheated uncovered.

SERVES 4-6

LEMON AND ROSEMARY CHICKEN WITH POTATOES

CHICKEN AND PASTA BAKE

A delicious combination of pasta, chicken and vegetables which can be baked ahead of time.

375g (12 oz) PENNE, COOKED "AL DENTE"
4 BONELESS AND SKINLESS CHICKEN BREASTS
60ml (4 Tbs) BALSAMIC VINEGAR
60ml (4 Tbs) OLIVE OIL
SALT AND PEPPER

Marinate chicken breasts in vinegar and olive oil overnight. Season well. Pan fry in an olive oil sprayed pan until just cooked. Cut into thin strips after cooking. Set aside.

60ml (1/4 cup) OLIVE OIL
1 ONION, FINELY CHOPPED
10ml (2 tsps) MINCED GARLIC
15ml (1 Tbs) DRY ROSEMARY
4 x 400g (14 oz) CANS WHOLE PEELED TOMATOES, PURÉED WITH LIQUID
4 RED PEPPERS, GRILLED - 2 CHOPPED COARSELY and 2 CUT INTO STRIPS*
SUGAR, SALT & PEPPER TO TASTE

Sauté onion and garlic in olive oil until brown. Add rosemary and tomatoes and reduce on medium heat for about 10 minutes. Add sugar, salt and pepper to taste. Divide the tomato mixture into two. Stir the chopped red peppers into half (mix 1) and the strips into the other half (mix 2). Set aside.

250g (8 oz) MEDIUM BROWN MUSHROOMS, QUARTERED
10 SMALL BABY ONIONS
30ml (2 Tbs) OLIVE OIL
10ml (2 tsps) DRY ROSEMARY
SALT & PEPPER

Preheat oven to 180°C (375°F).
Place onions and mushrooms in a roasting pan. Sprinkle with olive oil, rosemary, salt & pepper and roast for approximately 20 minutes or until just cooked. Add mushrooms, onions and chicken strips to mix 2. Spray an open casserole with non-stick cooking spray. Spread a layer of mix 1 covering the bottom of the dish. Then spread a layer of penne. Top with mix 2. Cover with foil. Bake covered for 25-30 minutes or until heated through.

NOTE: This can be prepared ahead, refrigerated and baked just before serving for 25-30 minutes or until heated through.

* See appendix

SERVES 8

SWEET CHILLI CHINESE CHICKEN WITH NOODLES

This makes a very colourful and delicious stir-fry served on a bed of noodles.

250g (8 oz) THIN NOODLES or EGG NOODLES, BOILED AND THEN FRIED IN BATCHES IN OIL UNTIL CRISPY.

4-6 BONELESS & SKINLESS CHICKEN BREASTS

30ml (2 Tbs) OLIVE OIL
1 ONION, SLICED THINLY
250g (8 oz) MUSHROOMS, SLICED
2 STICKS CELERY, VERY THINLY SLICED
2 SPRING ONIONS, THINLY SLICED
1 YELLOW PEPPER, CUT INTO THIN STRIPS
1 RED PEPPER, CUT INTO THIN STRIPS
1 BUNCH BOK CHOY, THICKLY SLICED

Cut breasts into thin strips. Place in a small bowl, season with salt and pepper and toss with 1 Tbs olive oil. Heat remaining oil in wok and fry onion until golden. Remove. Add chicken pieces and stir-fry in batches until browned for a few minutes on each side. Remove and add to onion. Stir-fry mushrooms until dry, seasoning with salt and pepper. Remove and add to chicken and onion.
Stir-fry celery, spring onion and peppers for a few seconds. Remove.

SAUCE
125ml (1/2 cup) PINEAPPLE JUICE*
60ml (1/4 cup) SOYA SAUCE
45ml (3 Tbs) TOMATO SAUCE
15ml (1 Tbs) HONEY
60ml (1/4 cup) SWEET CHILLI SAUCE**
30ml (2 Tbs) LEMON JUICE

15-30ml (1-2 Tbs) MAIZENA (CORNSTARCH), DISSOLVED IN COLD WATER

Pour sauce ingredients into wok and boil rapidly, thickening with maizena. Place everything back in wok, including the bok choy and stir-fry until well coated and vegetables are cooked.

Place noodles on serving platter and top with chicken and vegetables just before serving.

* Drain canned pineapple, or crushed pineapple for juice
** See sauces - bottled or homemade

SERVES 8-10

SWEET CHILLI CHINESE CHICKEN W TH NOODLES

CHICKEN AND VEGETABLE RISOTTO

I love making a dish which combines chicken and vegetables. This is particularly delicious.

4 CHICKEN BREASTS, CUT INTO STRIPS
60ml ($^1/_4$ cup) OLIVE OIL

1 ONION, CHOPPED
5ml (1 tsp) MINCED GARLIC
2 CARROTS, CHOPPED
500ml (2 cups) ARBORIO (Italian Rice)
250ml (1 cup) WHITE WINE
625ml (2$^1/_2$ cups) CHICKEN STOCK
(3 KNORR or 4 TELMA CUBES DISSOLVED)
20g ($^1/_2$ oz) DRIED PORCINI MUSHROOMS*
3 TOMATOES, DICED
6 ZUCCHINI, CUT IN SLICES AND THEN HALVED
125ml ($^1/_2$ cup) FROZEN PETIT POIS
125ml ($^1/_2$ cup) CORN KERNELS
30ml (2 Tbs) CHOPPED PARSLEY
5ml (1 tsp) DRY SAGE
SALT AND PEPPER

* Soak dry porcini mushrooms in 175ml ($^3/_4$ cup) boiling water for about 10 minutes.

Preheat oven to 200°C (400°F).

Sauté chicken breasts in 30ml (2 Tbs) olive oil until seared and half-cooked. Set aside.
In same pot, sauté onion, garlic and carrots in remaining olive oil until golden. Add dry uncooked rice and sauté for a few minutes, stirring constantly.

Mix white wine, chicken stock and liquid of the porcini mushrooms together. Slowly pour 1$^1/_2$ cups of this liquid into the rice, stirring all the time ensuring that the rice absorbs it.

After a few minutes add soaked porcini, zucchini and corn. Pour remaining liquid over rice and vegetables. Stir in parsley, sage and lots of seasoning. Toss in the cooked chicken.

Place everything into an ovenproof casserole with a lid, and bake for 25 mins. or until rice has softened and cooked through and almost all of the liquid has been absorbed. Stir in tomatoes and petit pois. Serve immediately.

SERVES 8

SESAME NOODLE AND CHICKEN STIR-FRY

A delicious combination of chicken and sesame seeds using leftover cooked chicken.

750ml (3 cups) SHREDDED, COOKED CHICKEN
1 BUNCH SPRING ONIONS, FINELY SLICED
$^1/_2$ ENGLISH CUCUMBER, SEEDS REMOVED AND SLICED VERY THINLY
1 BUNCH TAH TSAI, SLICED*
300g (9 oz) BEAN SPROUTS
OLIVE OIL

200g (7 oz) ANGEL-HAIR PASTA PRECOOKED (optional)
45ml (3 Tbs) TOASTED SESAME SEEDS**

SAUCE
15ml (1 Tbs) SESAME OIL***
45ml (3 Tbs) OLIVE OIL
30ml (2 Tbs) APPLE CIDER VINEGAR or RICE VINEGAR
5ml (1 tsp) CHILLI PASTE or POWDER
5ml (1 tsp) MINCED GARLIC
80ml ($^1/_3$ cup) SOYA SAUCE
45ml (3 Tbs) HONEY
SALT AND PEPPER

Mix all sauce ingredients together.

Heat wok. Sauté spring onion in a little olive oil. Add shredded chicken, cucumber, tah tsai and bean sprouts and stir-fry quickly.

Add sauce to wok and stir-fry with vegetables and chicken, until mixed through.

Heat the noodles and toss with sesame seeds.

Place noodles on a platter and top with vegetables and chicken. Serve immediately.

* Tah Tsai - Chinese spinach
** To toast sesame seeds - place dry on a baking tray in a preheated 140°C (325°F) oven for 10 minutes.
*** See sauces

SERVES 4-6

CHICKEN AND VEGETABLE RISOTTO

TANDOORI CHICKEN

The spices in the sauce give the chicken a wonderful yellow colour and slightly curried taste which is enhanced by the sambal accompaniment.

1kg (2.2 lbs) CHICKEN PIECES

SAUCE
5ml (1 tsp) TURMERIC
5ml (1 tsp) CORIANDER
10ml (2 tsps) CUMIN
1 ONION, CHOPPED FINELY
5ml (1 tsp) MINCED GARLIC
5ml (1 tsp) GROUND GINGER
2.5ml (½ tsp) CHILLI PASTE or POWDER
15ml (1 Tbs) LEMON RIND, FINELY GRATED
JUICE OF 1 LEMON
5ml (1 tsp) CHICKEN STOCK POWDER
30ml (2 Tbs) TOMATO SAUCE
250ml (1 cup) COCONUT MILK

Preheat oven to 180°C (375°F).

Mix all sauce ingredients together. Pour over chicken and marinate for 24 hours before cooking.

Place chicken in a small roasting pan, and roast skin side down, uncovered for 15 minutes, basting continuously. Turn and roast a further 15 minutes. Then turn on grill and brown each side for the remaining 15 -20 minutes of cooking.

Chicken pieces will take about 45 minutes to cook.

Serve with some basmati rice, and tomato, onion and mint sambal.

TOMATO, ONION & MINT SAMBAL
2 TOMATOES, CHOPPED, WITH SKIN
½ SMALL ONION, CHOPPED
30ml (2 Tbs) FRESH MINT, CHOPPED
COARSE SALT
PEPPER

Mix all ingredients together.

NOTE: Chicken can be prepared in advance and reheated uncovered.

SERVES 4-6

CASHEW CHICKEN WITH OYSTER MUSHROOMS

I love a stir-fry with a sauce that coats the chicken and the vegetables. The noodles can either be stir-fried with the chicken or placed on a platter and topped with the chicken and vegetables.

8 CHICKEN BREASTS, SKIN ON, BONE REMOVED
100g (3½ oz) UNSALTED CASHEW NUTS
30ml (2 Tbs) OLIVE OIL
6 SPRING ONIONS, CUT ON DIAGONAL
250g (8 oz) OYSTER MUSHROOMS (FRESH)
175g (4½ oz) FRESH SPINACH, COARSELY SHREDDED

250g (8 oz) PREBOILED NOODLES or EGG NOODLES

SAUCE
175ml (¾ cup) SOYA SAUCE
80ml (⅓ cup) KOSHER SWEET WINE or
MEDIUM CREAM SHERRY
125ml (½ cup) TOMATO SAUCE
30ml (2 Tbs) APPLE CIDER VINEGAR or
RICE VINEGAR
30ml (2 Tbs) TREACLE BROWN SUGAR
20ml (2 dessertspoons) BARBEQUE SAUCE
80ml (⅓ cup) APRICOT JAM

Season chicken breasts very well with spices and place skin-side up on a foil-lined baking tray under grill for 8 minutes. Remove from oven and cut into 4 pieces.

Heat oil in wok and lightly sauté spring onions and cashews until toasted. Set aside. Sauté oyster mushrooms for 1 minute each side, remove from wok and add to cashews and spring onions.

Mix all sauce ingredients together. Pour into wok and boil on high until slightly thickened.

Add chicken pieces and spinach and sauté until well coated and chicken is cooked. Add cashews, onions and mushrooms.

Serve immediately.

SERVES 12-15

TANDOORI CHICKEN

CASHEW CHICKEN WITH OYSTER MUSHROOMS

TURKEY WITH ROASTED APPLE SAUCE

The turkey has a marvellous apple and ginger taste, and is gorgeous, brown and crispy when roasted.

6kg (13.2 lbs) TURKEY

6 RED or GREEN APPLES, CUT INTO WEDGES WITH SKIN ON
5ml (1 tsp) GROUND GINGER
SALT AND PEPPER
OLIVE OIL

500ml (2 cups) ORANGE JUICE
2 TELMA CHICKEN or 1 KNORR STOCK CUBES
175ml (3/4 cup) APPLE SAUCE
5ml (1 tsp) GROUND GINGER

Preheat oven to 200°C (400°F).

Place apple wedges in a large roasting pan. Season with salt, pepper and ginger. Drizzle with a drop of olive oil. Roast until well browned on both sides, shaking pan every 10 minutes for about 30 minutes. Remove.

Place turkey in same roasting pan and season very generously with salt and pepper. Roast on 180°C (375°F) for at least 1 1/2 hours until well browned and golden on all sides.

In the meantime, place orange juice in a pot and reduce on high heat until you have 1 1/2 cups. Add the chicken stock cubes and apple sauce. Pour this mixture into the roasting pan over the turkey, mixing it with the turkey juices at the bottom of the pan. Return roasted apples to pan and continue to cook both for another 45 minutes.

Should you need more gravy, add a little boiling water to the roasting pan. Add extra salt if desired. Carve turkey and serve sauce separately or spoon sauce over turkey to prevent it from drying out.

NOTE: Turkey can be made several days ahead and refrigerated until ready to use. Bring to room temperature. Reheat uncovered on 160°C (350°F) for at least 45 minutes or longer.

SERVES 20

COQ AU VIN

My family says this is the best Coq au Vin they have ever tasted! (It is also the "only" Coq au Vin they have ever tasted)

2 X WHOLE CHICKENS, CUT INTO PIECES
750ml (3 cups) GOOD QUALITY RED WINE
4 BAY LEAVES
SALT AND PEPPER
FRESH THYME SPRIGS

250g (8 oz) PEELED BABY ONIONS, BLANCHED*
500g (1 lb) MUSHROOMS, WHOLE
200g (7 oz) BABY CARROTS, PEELED

125ml (1/2 cup) BRANDY
30ml (2 Tbs) FLOUR
30ml (2 Tbs) WATER
750ml (3 cups) CHICKEN STOCK (3 TELMA or 2 KNORR CUBES)
45ml (3 Tbs) TOMATO PURÉE
45ml (3 Tbs) CHOPPED PARSLEY

Marinate the chicken pieces overnight in the wine with the bay leaves, thyme, salt and pepper. Next day remove the chicken from the marinade and pat dry, retaining the marinade.

Season chicken and sauté in a large non-stick pot in batches until well browned. Set aside.

Brown blanched baby onions in the same pot. Add to the chicken pieces. Then place the mushrooms and carrots in the pot and sauté them until slightly browned. Add to the chicken as well.

Deglaze (boil very quickly on high) the brandy in the same pot, whisk in the flour (mixed to a paste with the water) to thicken the sauce. Add the chicken stock and bring to a boil. Then add the reserved marinade, tomato purée and parsley and boil on a high heat until thickened and slightly reduced.

When the sauce is reduced, place chicken pieces and vegetables back into the pot and allow to simmer for about 45-50 minutes. Remove the lid and boil uncovered for a thicker sauce.

* Bring a pot of water to a boil. Boil onions for 5 minutes.

SERVES 8-10

TURKEY WITH ROASTED APPLE SAUCE

EGGPLANT ROLLATINI

Vegetables

HERBED POTATO MEDLEY

EGGPLANT ROLLATINI

POTATO TART

GLAZED ROASTED BABY ONIONS

Vegetables

Vegeta

Many of us could live on vegetables alone. They are fresh, delicious and quite beautiful and range from gourmet baby vegetables to exotic mushrooms to absolutely perfect baby red peppers. Wonderful assortments of fresh herbs add aroma and superb flavour to these vegetables in whatever form they are presented.

My favourite way of serving is on large platters using a medley of whatever's in season. I chop and change as the seasons come and go, adapting and varying recipes to suit the occasion, cooking them in as many different ways as possible. Roasting at very high temperatures or grilling on a pan adds colour and a special taste to them. The use of freshly ground coarse salt or salt crystals and fresh black pepper brings out the basic taste, and my all-time favourite seasoning is of course, Herbamare (a natural seasoning available in health shops worldwide) and which adds a new dimension to the veggies.

Vegetables absorb a lot of seasoning, so indulge and overdo it a bit to give them flavour. Drizzles of fragrant olive oil and freshly chopped herbs make vegetable platters absolutely wonderful to both the eye and the palate. It is also an easy way to suit all tastes, as people will choose whatever vegetables they prefer. I find it amazing that non-vegetable eaters suddenly transform into "pseudo-vegetarians" when presented with vegetables served this way.

Remember to allow for a certain amount of shrinkage with both vegetable and starch dishes (like potatoes), so your quantities will be quite a lot less at the end. The myriad of sauces in this section accompanying all the recipes will tickle your taste buds.

lles

QUICK AND EASY

- STIR-FRY SLICED VEGETABLES
- PUMPKIN PIE
- BAKED ASSORTED PUMPKIN WEDGES
- GRILLED MUSHROOM KEBABS

RECIPES

- BASMATI RICE PILAF
- SWEET POTATO LATKES
- TARTARE MASH POTATOES
- HERBED POTATO MEDLEY
- ROASTED VEGETABLE TART WITH SWEET ONION MARMALADE
- MUSHROOM AND BUTTERNUT PHYLLO ROLLS
- ROASTED VEGETABLE STRUDEL
- STEAMED VEGETABLES WITH SESAME SEEDS
- EGGPLANT ROLLATINI
- POTATO TART
- TROPICAL ASIAN CURRY VEGETABLES
- PARSLEY AND LIME MASHED POTATOES
- STIR-FRIED RICE
- GLAZED ROASTED BABY ONIONS
- ROASTED POTATO WEDGES
- ROASTED BABY VEGETABLES WITH LEMONGRASS OIL

Vegetables

STIR-FRY SLICED VEGETABLES

3 MEDIUM CARROTS, SLICED
200g (7 oz) BABY GEMS
125g (4 oz) BABY YELLOW PATTY PANS
125g (4 oz) ZUCCHINI
125g (4 oz) MUSHROOMS, SLICED
OLIVE OIL
SALT, PEPPER AND HERBAMARE

Heat a little olive oil in a wok. Slice carrots thinly and stir-fry on high heat for a few minutes, seasoning with salt and pepper.

Slice remaining vegetables in rounds very thinly and add to carrots, seasoning well with herbamare. Stir-fry until just cooked. Set aside until ready to serve.

NOTE: Vegetables can be half-cooked, then reheated in the microwave on high to complete the cooking. Season generously before serving.

SERVES 4

PUMPKIN PIE

1kg (2.2 lbs) PUMPKIN CHUNKS
250ml (1 cup) FLOUR
60ml (4 Tbs) MARGARINE or BUTTER (MELTED)
60-80ml ($^1/_4$ - $^1/_3$ cup) SUGAR
10ml (2 tsps) BAKING POWDER
3 EGGS
5ml (1 tsp) SALT
250ml (1 cup) CREAM or NON-DAIRY CREAMER

Preheat oven to 180°C (375°F).

Cook pumpkin on high in microwave in a little water for at least 10 minutes or until very soft. Drain well, mash and mix with remaining ingredients. Place in a pre-sprayed quiche dish and bake for 1 hour or until set.

NOTE: Can be made ahead, refrigerated until ready to bake and then baked. Sugar can be adjusted depending on taste i.e. begin with less and add more if necessary.

SERVES 8-10

BAKED ASSORTED PUMPKIN WEDGES

1kg (2.2 lbs) PUMPKIN, PEELED AND CUT INTO THIN WEDGES **or**
1kg (2.2 lbs) ASSORTMENT OF BABY PUMPKINS (JACK-BE-LITTLE, HUBBARD SQUASH,
SWEET DUMPLINGS AND GOLDEN NUGGETS),
UNPEELED AND CUT INTO THIN WEDGES
OLIVE OIL SPRAY
COARSE SALT, HERBAMARE AND BLACK PEPPER
HONEY or CINNAMON SUGAR

Preheat oven to 200°C (400°F).

Place squashes and pumpkins on foil-lined baking trays and spray with olive oil spray. Season generously.

Bake uncovered for 20 mins or until slightly softened. Turn over, spray once more with olive oil spray and season. Bake a further 20 minutes or until just softened.

Just before serving, sprinkle with cinnamon-sugar or drizzle with a little honey.

SERVES 4-6

GRILLED MUSHROOM KEBABS

20 MEDIUM - LARGE MUSHROOMS
WOODEN KEBAB STICKS
75ml (5 Tbs) FRESH SAGE, CHOPPED
75ml (5 Tbs) FRESH OREGANO, CHOPPED
JUICE OF 2 LEMONS
60ml ($^1/_4$ cup) OLIVE OIL
SALT AND PEPPER

Preheat oven to 180°C (375°F). Place mushrooms cap side up in a roasting pan. Sprinkle with chopped sage, oregano, a drizzle of olive oil and a good squeeze of lemon juice. Season generously. Marinate for a few hours if possible to allow flavour to absorb.

Remove mushrooms from marinade and thread 4-5 on long kebab sticks. Drizzle with remaining marinade and squeeze with more lemon juice. Season again.

Bake for 20-25 mins. Remove from oven and grill lightly just before serving.

NOTE: Mushrooms shrink a lot when roasting, so buy larger ones to allow for shrinkage.

SERVES 6

BASMATI RICE PILAF

625ml ($2\frac{1}{2}$ cups) BASMATI RICE
875ml ($3\frac{1}{2}$ cups) COLD WATER (3 TELMA or 2 KNORR CHICKEN CUBES)
30ml (2 Tbs) OLIVE OIL
1 ONION CHOPPED FINELY
250g (8 oz) MUSHROOMS, CHOPPED COARSELY
30ml (2 Tbs) SOYA SAUCE
80ml ($\frac{1}{3}$ cup) CHOPPED PARSLEY
125ml ($\frac{1}{2}$ cup) FLAKED ALMONDS, TOASTED

Place uncooked rice, cold water and stock cubes in a large pot and bring to a boil. Reduce heat to low and simmer for 18 mins. Remove from stove and leave in pot with lid on for 5 minutes to complete the cooking (off the stove).

Sauté the onions in the olive oil. Add mushrooms and sauté until dry. Mix with cooked rice.

Stir in soya sauce, parsley and toasted flaked almonds just before serving.

NOTE: Can be frozen, defrosted and reheated in microwave.

SERVES 8-10

SWEET POTATO LATKES

4 LARGE SWEET POTATOES, COARSELY GRATED
1 ONION, COARSELY GRATED
30ml (2 Tbs) FLOUR
SALT AND PEPPER

Place the grated sweet potato and onion in a strainer and squeeze out any excess water.
Mix with flour, salt and pepper.

Heat a little oil in a frying pan until medium-hot. Place small balls of mixture into the oil and flatten with a fork. Fry until golden and crispy on both sides.

Drain on paper towels. Be careful not to burn. Keep uncovered until ready to use, or they will be soggy.

Reheat in 120°C (300°F) oven for 10 minutes uncovered on a baking rack.

MAKES ± 30

TARTARE MASH POTATOES

3 LARGE BAKING POTATOES
45ml (3 Tbs) BUTTER
500ml (2 cups) MILK
SALT, PEPPER, HERBAMARE
30ml (2 Tbs) CHOPPED PARSLEY
30ml (2 Tbs) CHOPPED RED PEPPER

Boil peeled potatoes until soft. Mash and add butter, milk and seasoning.

Mix in parsley and red pepper.

Can be made ahead and refrigerated until ready to use. Reheat as required covered in the microwave.

SERVES 6

HERBED POTATO MEDLEY

30 BABY POTATOES, CUT IN HALF WITH SKIN ON
6 SMALL-MEDIUM SWEET POTATOES, CUT INTO CHUNKS WITH SKIN ON
45ml (3 Tbs) FRESH ROSEMARY, CHOPPED
45ml (3 Tbs) FRESH OREGANO, CHOPPED
10 SPRIGS OF THYME, STEM REMOVED
OLIVE OIL
COARSE SALT AND PEPPER

Preheat oven to 200°C (400°F).

Mix rosemary, oregano, thyme, salt and pepper in a bowl. Sprinkle liberally over the potatoes and sweet potatoes in a large roasting pan. Drizzle with a little olive oil.

Bake on bottom rack until golden, shaking pan all the time. Roast for about 1 hour.

NOTE: Potatoes shrink when roasted.

SERVES 10-12

ROASTED VEGETABLE TART WITH SWEET ONION MARMALADE

This is a glorious, colourful tart topped and sweetened by the onions. It can be made ahead in different parts, assembled and baked before serving.

SWEET ONION MARMALADE
30ml (2 Tbs) OLIVE OIL
4 RED ONIONS, SLICED
2.5ml (1/2 tsp) GARLIC
2 BAY LEAVES
250ml (1 cup) WATER
30ml (2 Tbs) RED WINE VINEGAR
45ml (3 Tbs) HONEY
45ml (3 Tbs) TREACLE BROWN SUGAR
SALT

Sauté onions, garlic and bay leaves in olive oil over low heat until very soft for about 15-20 minutes. Add water and simmer until liquid is reduced. Add vinegar, honey, brown sugar and a little salt. Simmer until most of the liquid has evaporated not allowing the onions to become too dry. Set aside to cool.

ROASTED VEGETABLES
1 EGGPLANT, DICED
4 ZUCCHINI, SLICED
5 YELLOW PATTY PANS, SLICED
5 BABY GEMS, SLICED
15ml (1 Tbs) FRESH THYME, CHOPPED
15ml (1 Tbs) FRESH ROSEMARY, CHOPPED
10ml (2 tsps) WHOLEGRAIN MUSTARD
SALT, PEPPER, HERBAMARE
30ml (2 Tbs) OLIVE OIL

Preheat oven to 200°C (400°F). Place all vegetables in a roasting pan, tossed with fresh herbs, mustard and olive oil. Season well. Roast for 20-30 mins until almost cooked. Set aside.

200g (7 oz) PUFF PASTRY
1 EGG, LIGHTLY BEATEN WITH A DROP OF WATER
2 WHOLE EGGS
125ml (1/2 cup) CREAM
175ml (3/4 cup) CRUMBLED FETA CHEESE

Roll out puff pastry into a circle (about 26cm - 10 inch), building up the sides in strips to form a shell. Brush each strip with beaten egg to stick pastry together. Place on baking paper or exopat on a baking tray, using toothpicks in corners to hold them down. Bake for 20 minutes.

Reduce temp of oven to 180°C (375°F) Fill pastry case with vegetables. Top with caramelised onions. Beat eggs with cream and pour over. Bake for 20 mins. Sprinkle with crumbled feta and bake for another 10 mins. Serve immediately.

SERVES 8-10

MUSHROOM AND BUTTERNUT PHYLLO ROLLS

There is nothing nicer than light pastry filled with vegetables, which are full of taste and colour. This makes a stunning accompaniment to any dish.

500g (1 lb) MUSHROOMS, CHOPPED COARSELY
500g (1 1/2 cups) RAW BUTTERNUT, PEELED AND GRATED COARSELY
30ml (2 Tbs) MARGARINE or BUTTER
22ml (1 1/2 Tbs) FLOUR
125ml (1/2 cup) VEGETABLE STOCK
(1/2 TELMA PAREVE CHICKEN STOCK CUBE or 1/2 KNORR CUBE)
30ml (2 Tbs) CHIVES, CHOPPED
45ml (3 Tbs) ITALIAN PARSLEY, CHOPPED
SALT AND PEPPER

Preheat oven to 180°C (375°F).

Fry mushrooms until dry. Add butternut and sauté for a few minutes. Season. Remove and set aside.

In the same pan, melt margarine or butter. Stir in flour and cook for 1 min. Whisk and add stock. Allow to thicken. Return vegetables to frying pan and mix well. Season to taste.

Stir in the chives and Italian parsley.

Spray 2 sheets of phyllo each with olive oil spray. Stack them on top of one another. Cut each sheet of phyllo into 4. Place a little mixture along one side of each phyllo quarter and roll up like a cigar. Continue until all filling is used.

Place rolls on an exopat mat or foil-lined baking tray, spray with more olive oil and bake for 20 minutes.

NOTE: These can be made ahead and refrigerated covered with plastic wrap until ready to bake.

SERVES 8

ROASTED VEGETABLE TART WITH SWEET ONION MARMALADE

ROASTED VEGETABLE STRUDEL

There is nothing nicer than beautifully roasted vegetables in layers with a little cheese, all wrapped up in phyllo.

5 SHEETS PHYLLO
UNSALTED BUTTER AND OLIVE OIL SPRAY

125g (4 oz) INA PAARMAN SUN-DRIED TOMATO PESTO (or ANY TOMATO PESTO)
1 EGGPLANT, SLICED AND ROASTED*
250g (8 oz) ZUCCHINI, CUT INTO THIN STRIPS AND ROASTED*
250g (8 oz) MEDIUM BROWN MUSHROOMS, ROASTED AND THEN SLICED*
FEW BASIL LEAVES
300g (9 oz) HALOUMI CHEESE, GRATED
TOASTED SESAMI SEEDS

Preheat oven to 180°C (375°F).

Brush alternate sheets of phyllo with butter and remaining sheets with olive oil spray. Stack them on top of each other.

Brush a little sun-dried tomato pesto on the top sheet of phyllo. Then sprinkle some of the grated cheese down centre of sheet. Layer vegetables in a long row down the centre of the phyllo on top of the cheese. Top with more cheese and dollops of pesto.

Roll up to make a strudel and pinch edges together, placing seam side down. Brush or spray outside of strudel with olive oil spray and sprinkle with toasted sesame seeds.

Place on baking paper or on an exopat mat on a baking tray and bake for 30 minutes or until golden.

NOTE: Can be made ahead, refrigerated covered with plastic wrap until ready to bake. Do not freeze.

*To roast vegetables: Preheat oven to 220°C (440°F). Line a large baking tray with foil and spray with olive oil spray. Place vegetables in rows down the width of the baking tray. Spray them with olive oil spray and season very well with herbamare, salt and pepper. Roast for 10 minutes or until softened and golden, turning once.

SERVES 8-10

STEAMED VEGETABLES WITH SESAME SEEDS

When steaming vegetables their glorious colours emerge and they have a special flavour. These can be served with the sauce and sesame seeds, or just steamed on their own. Either way, there is nothing nicer than a perfectly steamed vegetable.

1 LEMON, PARSLEY SPRIGS, 2 STALKS LEMONGRASS

ASSORTED VEGETABLES
200g (7 oz) FINE FRENCH GREEN BEANS
200g (7 oz) BABY CARROTS
250g (8 oz) YELLOW PATTY PANS, CUT IN HALF
250g (8 oz) THIN FRESH GREEN ASPARAGUS
250g (8 oz) FROZEN or FRESH BROCCOLI FLORETS
125g (4 oz) SNOW PEAS

SAUCE
30ml (2 Tbs) TREACLE BROWN SUGAR
15ml (1 Tbs) WHOLEGRAIN MUSTARD
60ml (1/4 cup) BALSAMIC VINEGAR
80ml (1/3 cup) OLIVE OIL
SALT AND PEPPER

Whisk all sauce ingredients together. Set aside until ready to use.

TOASTED SESAME SEEDS
Toast seeds on a baking tray in a preheated 140°C (325°F) oven for 10 minutes.
Set aside.

Place a bamboo steamer in a pot, or over a wok with a little water at the bottom. Squeeze some lemon juice, add a few parsley sprigs and 2 stalks of lemongrass to the water.

As the water boils, place the beans, carrots and patty pans in the steamer for 5 minutes, seasoning generously with salt, pepper and herbamare.
After 3 minutes add the asparagus, broccoli and lastly the snow peas, seasoning as well. These only need 2-3 minutes.

NOTE: Always steam the hardest vegetables first and then add the vegetables which require less time.

Remove them from the steamer, place on serving platter and drizzle with sauce. Sprinkle with toasted sesame seeds and serve immediately.

SERVES 8

ROASTED VEGETABLE STRUDEL

EGGPLANT ROLLATINI

This is one of those wonderful, delicious and tasty eggplant dishes with a separate sauce, which vegetarians will go mad about. It also looks as good as it tastes.

4 LONG EGGPLANTS
250ml (1 cup) RICOTTA or LOW FAT CHUNKY COTTAGE CHEESE
250g (8 oz) FETA CHEESE
125ml ($^1/_2$ cup) PARMESAN, GRATED (or EXTRA FETA OR HALOUMI)
60ml (4 Tbs) FRESHLY CHOPPED BASIL
175ml ($^3/_4$ cup) MOZZARELLA, GRATED
OLIVE OIL
SALT AND PEPPER

Slice eggplant lengthwise. Place in a strainer and sprinkle with salt. Leave for 20 mins. Then rinse with cold water.

Preheat oven to 180°C (375°F).

Drizzle a little olive oil on a foil-lined baking tray. Arrange eggplant slices on foil, season with salt and pepper, brush with some more olive oil and grill for a few minutes on each side until softened and cooked. Set aside to cool.

Mix all cheeses and herbs together. Place a spoonful on each slice of eggplant and roll up. Lay in a sprayed ovenproof dish, with seam side down.

Bake for 30 mins uncovered or until warmed through with a little sauce drizzled over the middle of each eggplant roll.

SAUCE
30ml (2 Tbs) OLIVE OIL
125ml ($^1/_2$ cup) ONION, CHOPPED FINELY
5ml (1 tsp) MINCED GARLIC
2 x 400g (14 oz) CANS WHOLE PEELED TOMATOES (RETAIN LIQUID FROM 1 CAN)
125ml ($^1/_2$ cup) WHITE WINE (OPTIONAL) (or VEGETABLE STOCK)
10ml (2 tsps) SUGAR
15-30ml (1-2 Tbs) FRESH BASIL
SALT AND PEPPER

Sauté onion and garlic in olive oil until softened. Add tomatoes and wine (or stock) and simmer until thickened on medium heat uncovered to reduce slightly. Add sugar, salt, pepper and basil to taste.

Top rolls with more chopped basil just before serving.

NOTE: The eggplant rolls and the sauce can be made up to 2 days ahead and refrigerated covered with plastic. Bring to room temperature before baking.

SERVES 8-10

POTATO TART

This makes a delectable potato dish with a difference. It can be prepared and baked ahead and then reheated successfully before serving.

200g (7 oz) PUFF PASTRY
3 LARGE YELLOW, WAXY POTATOES, PEELED (MEDITERRANEAN)
OLIVE OIL SPRAY
1 EGG BEATEN
COARSE SALT AND PEPPER

Preheat oven to 200°C (400°F).

Boil potatoes until half-cooked (about 10 minutes).

Roll pastry into a circle to fit into the base and a little up the sides of a 26cm (10 inch) springform tin. Prick the bottom of the pastry with a fork and refrigerate for $^1/_2$ an hour.

Cut the potatoes into wedges, and arrange them in overlapping circles with the pointed side facing down, fanning them on top of the pastry. Spray with olive oil spray and season with salt and pepper.

Brush the edges of the pastry with beaten egg and slash them at intervals at an angle.

Bake for 20 minutes and then reduce the temperature to 180°C (375°F) and bake for a further 40-50 minutes or until golden.

SERVES 6-8

GRILLED MUSHROOM KEBABS

POTATC TART

TROPICAL ASIAN CURRY VEGETABLES

A medley of vegetables with a superb colour and taste, enhanced by the yellow curry paste. They can also be tossed with cooked angel-hair noodles.

CURRY PASTE
5ml (1 tsp) TURMERIC
15ml (1 Tbs) FRESH CORIANDER
5ml (1 tsp) MINCED BOTTLED GARLIC
2 STALKS LEMON GRASS
5ml (1 tsp) FRESH LIME JUICE (or BOTTLED LEMON JUICE)
1 MEDIUM ONION, CUT INTO PIECES
5ml (1 tsp) GROUND CUMIN
5ml (1 tsp) COARSE SALT (or MORE IF NECESSARY)
60ml ($^1/_4$ cup) OLIVE OIL
125ml ($^1/_2$ cup) COCONUT MILK*

Place all ingredients in a food processor and process to make a paste. Then add the coconut milk. This can be made ahead and kept in the fridge.

CHUNKS OF ASSORTED VEGETABLES
2 COOKED MIELIES or 250g (8 oz) BABY CORN
250g (8 oz) BUTTERNUT
1 SWEET POTATO
250g (8 oz) ZUCCHINI
250g (8 oz) BABY YELLOW PATTY PANS
250g (8 oz) BABY GEMS
250g (8 oz) MUSHROOMS
100g (3$^1/_2$ oz) BABY CARROTS, PEELED
125g (4 oz) FINE FRENCH GREEN BEANS
125g (4 oz) SNOW PEAS

Preheat oven to 220°C (440°F).

Place all vegetables (except beans and peas) in a single layer in a roasting pan and drizzle with a drop of olive oil. Season well with salt, pepper and herbamare. Roast uncovered for 20 minutes. Stir in curry paste, beans and peas and roast for another 20-25 minutes.

* see appendix

SERVES 6-8

PARSLEY AND LIME MASHED POTATOES

4 MEDIUM - LARGE BAKING POTATOES
15ml (1 Tbs) BUTTER or MARGARINE
175ml ($^3/_4$ cup) LOWFAT or SKIM MILK
COARSE SALT AND PEPPER
125ml ($^1/_2$ cup) FRESH PARSLEY, FINELY CHOPPED
RIND AND JUICE OF 1 LARGE LIME (IN SEASON) or LEMON RIND PLUS 3 Tbs BOTTLED LEMON JUICE

Peel and cut potatoes into chunks and cook in salted water until softened. Drain and mash adding butter and milk and mix until smooth.

Chop parsley very finely in food processor. Grate lime rind and add juice. Set aside.

Season potatoes very well. Add parsley, rind and lime juice. Stir until smooth.
Reheat in microwave when ready to serve.

SERVES 4-6

STIR-FRIED RICE

750ml (3 cups) COOKED JASMINE RICE (COLD)
45ml (3 Tbs) OLIVE OIL
3 EGGS, LIGHTLY BEATEN
30ml (2 Tbs) SOYA SAUCE
10ml (2 tsps) SALT
3 SPRING ONIONS (GREEN AND WHITE PART), FINELY CHOPPED
250ml (1 cup) FROZEN PETIT POIS, DEFROSTED

Heat oil in wok and scramble eggs until almost cooked through. Add cold rice and stir egg through quickly heating both.

Make a well in centre and add soya sauce, salt, spring onions and petit pois and stir-fry to coat rice. Adjust seasoning. Reheat in microwave, if desired.

TO COOK RICE
Wash rice very well 2-3 times. Place in a large pot with 3$^1/_4$ cups cold water and a pinch of salt. Bring to a boil. Turn stove down immediately to lowest setting. Cook with lid on for 15 mins. Take pot off stove, place a cloth under the lid allowing it to steam for 5-10 mins, then remove lid for rice to cool.

SERVES 8-10

TROPICAL ASIAN CURRY VEGETABLES

GLAZED ROASTED BABY ONIONS

A single vegetable drizzled with a sticky balsamic sauce completes this dish.

15 WHOLE BABY ONIONS, UNPEELED

60ml ($^{1}/_{4}$ cup) OLIVE OIL
60ml ($^{1}/_{4}$ cup) TREACLE BROWN SUGAR
80ml ($^{1}/_{3}$ cup) BALSAMIC VINEGAR
SALT AND PEPPER

Preheat oven to 180°C (375°F).

Boil baby onions with the skin on for about 45 minutes. When cool, peel them and place in a small sprayed roasting pan. Drizzle with olive oil, brown sugar, balsamic vinegar, salt and pepper.

Roast for about 1-1$^{1}/_{2}$ hours or until golden and well caramelised and glazed, basting continuously. Allow to cool before refrigerating.

NOTE: Reheat if necessary just before serving.

SERVES 4-6

ROASTED POTATO WEDGES

6-8 LARGE POTATOES, CUT LENGTHWISE INTO WEDGES, SKIN ON

10ml (2 tsps) ONION SALT
10ml (2 tsps) GARLIC SALT
5ml (1 tsp) SUGAR
5ml (1 tsp) PAPRIKA
5ml (1 tsp) HERBAMARE
2.5ml ($^{1}/_{2}$ tsp) CAYENNE PEPPER
COARSE SALT
BLACK PEPPER
OLIVE OIL

Preheat oven to 200°C (400°F).

Place potatoes skin side down in a large roasting pan. Mix all seasonings together and sprinkle generously over potatoes. Drizzle with a little olive oil. Bake until crispy and brown for about 1 hour, shaking pan occasionally.

SERVES 6

ROASTED BABY VEGETABLES WITH LEMONGRASS OIL

The aroma of lemongrass gives a subtle glaze and flavour to these beautiful baby vegetables which are roasted whole to retain their shape. Should they not be available, substitute with any others.

125g (4 oz) EACH OF THE FOLLOWING VEGETABLES*

BABY CARROTS
BABY YELLOW PATTY PANS
BABY BUTTERNUTS
WHOLE BABY BUTTON MUSHROOMS
BABY ZUCCHINI
BABY EGGPLANT
BABY GEMS
OLIVE OIL
4 SPRIGS OF FRESH THYME
COARSE SALT, PEPPER AND HERBAMARE

Preheat oven to 220°C (440°F).

Drizzle a little olive oil on the bottom of a roasting pan and place all the vegetables in one flat layer. Drizzle with a little more oil. Season generously with salt, pepper and herbamare. Dot with fresh sprigs of thyme. Roast for 30 minutes on the bottom rack of oven. Shake the roasting pan gently to mix vegetables and roast for a further 10-15 minutes.

Toss with lemongrass oil just before serving.

LEMONGRASS OIL
2 STICKS LEMONGRASS
15ml (1 Tbs) SUGAR
2 SPRING ONIONS, CHOPPED
60ml ($^{1}/_{4}$ cup) OLIVE OIL
30ml (2 Tbs) WHITE WINE VINEGAR
COARSE SALT

Remove hard outer leaves of the lemongrass stalk. Chop up the inner white part and place in food processor with remaining ingredients. Process until finely chopped. Adjust seasoning.

NOTE: Sauce can be made ahead and refrigerated for up to 1 week before using. Drizzle over roasted vegetables before serving.

* There are very small "gourmet" vegetables available in many of the local supermarkets.

SERVES 6-8

ROASTED BABY VEGETABLES WITH LEMONGRASS OIL

GLAZED ROASTED BABY ONIONS

FRUITY ICE CREAM PARFAIT

Desserts

BANANA SPLIT STRUDEL

FLOATING ISLAND

BAKLAVA ICE CREAM LOAF

MANGO SORBET

Desserts

Desser

There seems to be a trend in desserts to be more fruity and less creamy. However, I can never resist a good old-fashioned, sinfully rich one. Each of these is more decadent than the next, so enjoy, enjoy!

A colourful display of fruits, or the perfect crème caramel complete a meal, and I have yet to meet anyone who can dispute that fact. You will adore the fruit ice creams, whether creamy or sorbet, as each has a distinctive, wonderful colour and taste. From mango to plum to pistachio to lemon, these are sure to be a hit all-round.

There are many non-dairy alternatives in this section for those who are lactose intolerant or for those who observe religious dietary laws. In South Africa we have American non-dairy alternatives called Rich's Whip Kream and Rich's Whip Kream Base, besides the local "Orly Whip" and "Instawhip". You might be able to use "Haddar" (USA and Australia), if available in your country. Should you be able to use Rich's, it is the creamiest and nicest alternative (especially in ice creams) to cream. However, it is very sweet, so you need to omit a little sugar in the recipe.

Rich's Whip Kream Base can be diluted 2 to 1 with water to make a non-dairy milk, which is perfect for custards and white sauces as it can be heated. However, if this is not available, be aware that some of the other alternatives cannot be heated successfully.

QUICK AND EASY

- GRILLED BANANAS WITH ORANGE SALSA
- FRUIT KEBAB FONDUE
- CARAMELISED PEARS

RECIPES

- GRILLED FRESH FRUIT WITH GINGER MASCARPONE
- STEAMED CHOCOLATE PUDDING
- GRILLED FIGS AND NECTARINES WITH VANILLA CUSTARD
- FRESH FRUIT IN REDUCED JUICE
- BERRY TIRAMISU FILLED PAVLOVA
- BANANA SPLIT STRUDEL
- CRÈME CARAMEL
- BANANA TARTE TATIN
- PLUM TART
- FRUITY ICE CREAM PARFAIT
- FLOATING ISLAND
- SHAVED MANGO TART
- LEMON, LIME AND LEMONGRASS ICE CREAM
- PISTACHIO ICE CREAM
- BAKLAVA ICE CREAM LOAF
- WATERMELON GRANITA
- MANGO SORBET
- PLUM SORBET
- FIG ICE CREAM

GRILLED BANANAS WITH ORANGE SALSA

10 BANANAS, SLICED LENGTHWISE
125ml (1/2 cup) FRESH ORANGE JUICE
TREACLE BROWN SUGAR FOR GRILLING

ORANGE SALSA
2 ORANGES, PEELED, SEGMENTED & COARSELY DICED
2 NAARTJIES or MANDARINS, PEELED, SEGMENTED AND COARSELY DICED
400g (14 oz) CAN MANGO SLICES, DICED &
125ml (1/2 cup) JUICE FROM CAN
60ml (1/4 cup) CASTOR SUGAR

Toss all salsa ingredients together. Set aside.

Preheat oven to 200°C (400°F).

Slice bananas lengthwise and place in an ovenproof dish. Pour orange juice over and allow to marinate. Just before serving, sprinkle with sugar and bake for 15 mins, then grill for 5 mins to brown the bananas.

Spoon orange salsa down centre of bananas just before serving.

SERVES 8-10

FRUIT KEBAB FONDUE

CHUNKS OF FRUIT - STRAWBERRIES, BANANA, PINEAPPLE, PAPINO, MELONS

Assemble chunks of fruit onto kebab sticks, add the banana last to avoid it going brown.

STRAWBERRY SAUCE
250g (8 oz) STRAWBERRIES or MIXED BERRIES
CASTOR SUGAR

Purée strawberries or mixed berries in food processor. Depending on the sweetness of the fruit, add some castor sugar to sweeten.

CHOCOLATE SAUCE
200g (7 oz) DARK CHOCOLATE
30ml (2 Tbs) MARGARINE or BUTTER
175ml (3/4 cup) CREAM or NON-DAIRY CREAM

Melt the chocolate in microwave or in double boiler. Add the margarine or butter and then the cream or non-dairy cream. Stir to dissolve and mix everything well. Serve warm, not hot.

TO SERVE: Pile kebabs decoratively on a platter. Serve the chocolate sauce and strawberry sauce separately and each person will dip fruit into the sauces.

ACCOMPANIMENTS: Serve with sorbet or ice cream.

MAKES AS MANY AS YOU WANT

HANDY TIP: Dip whole banana with skin into boiling water for 1 min. to avoid turning brown, then peel.

CARAMELISED PEARS

8-10 BROWN BOSC PEARS
125ml (1/2 cup) TREACLE BROWN SUGAR
375ml (1 1/2 cups) CREAM
30ml (2 Tbs) LEMON JUICE

NON - DAIRY ALTERNATIVE:
8-10 BROWN BOSC PEARS
125ml (1/2 cup) TREACLE BROWN SUGAR
250ml (1 cup) NON-DAIRY CREAM
30ml (2 Tbs) LEMON JUICE

Preheat oven to 180°C (375°F).

Cut pears into quarters and place in a sprayed casserole dish.

Sprinkle them with sugar. Pour over cream or non-dairy cream and lemon juice and bake uncovered for 30 mins.

SERVES 6-8

WATERMELON GRANITA

GRILLED FRESH FRUIT SERVED WITH GINGER MASCARPONE

A glorious, colourful array of fresh fruits served warm or at room temperature which are complemented by the sexy combination of ginger and mascarpone - calories here we come!

MEDLEY OF ASSORTED FRESH FRUIT:
1 PINEAPPLE, CUT INTO CHUNKS
2 ORANGES
2 KIWI, PEELED AND CUT INTO THIRDS
250g (8 oz) STRAWBERRIES, WHOLE
2 PEARS, UNPEELED
2 BANANAS, CUT INTO CHUNKS
2 GUAVAS, UNPEELED
2 APPLES, UNPEELED
3 NECTARINES, UNPEELED
3 PEACHES, UNPEELED

175ml ($^3/_4$ cup) CASTOR SUGAR MIXED WITH VANILLA SEEDS FROM A VANILLA BEAN

Cut whole fruit into halves and quarters leaving skin on. Preheat grill in oven.

Place all fruit in a large roasting pan in one flat layer. Sprinkle with vanilla sugar.

Place in middle of the oven under the grill for 10 minutes or until sugar melts and fruit browns slightly. Watch carefully.

GINGER MASCARPONE
500ml (2 cups) MASCARPONE*
60ml ($^1/_4$ cup) CASTOR SUGAR
5ml (1 tsp) VANILLA ESSENCE
30ml (2 Tbs) PRESERVED GINGER SYRUP
12 GINGER BISCUITS, LIGHTLY CRUSHED

Mix mascarpone, castor sugar, vanilla essence and ginger syrup together. Just before serving stir in crushed ginger biscuit pieces.

TO SERVE: Serve mascarpone sauce as an accompaniment to the fruit.

* See appendix for mascarpone substitute

SERVES 8-10

STEAMED CHOCOLATE PUDDING

I have yet to meet anyone who does not love a sticky, warm, moist chocolate pudding. This one satisfies all those cravings. It is a perfect dessert for the whole family.

80ml ($^1/_3$ cup) MARGARINE or BUTTER
175ml ($^3/_4$ cup) SOFT BROWN SUGAR
30ml (2 Tbs) SYRUP
2 EGGS, SEPARATED
5ml (1 tsp) BICARBONATE OF SODA
125ml ($^1/_2$ cup) BOILING WATER
250ml (1 cup) FLOUR
2.5ml ($^1/_2$ tsp) SALT
5ml (1 tsp) BAKING POWDER
30ml (2 Tbs) COCOA
150g ($4^1/_2$ oz) GRATED DARK CHOCOLATE

Spray or grease a 1 litre (4 cup) ovenproof pudding bowl.

Fill a large pot $^1/_3$ full with water and bring to boil.

In a mixmaster cream margarine or butter, sugar and syrup together until light and fluffy. Add egg yolks one at a time and beat in very well.

Dissolve bicarbonate of soda in boiling water. Sift dry ingredients together and add to creamed mixture alternating with bicarbonate water.

Beat egg whites until stiff and fold into mixture.

Pour half batter into pudding bowl, sprinkle half of grated chocolate. Pour in remaining batter and sprinkle with remaining chocolate.

Cover with a double layer of wax paper and secure with string to cover the entire dish. Prick all over with a fork. Lower bowl into the pot of boiling water, cover pot with lid and simmer slowly for 1-$1^1/_2$ hours. DO NOT OPEN. Holding string, remove bowl from the water and cool.

NOTE: Warm slightly before removing from dish. Loosen with a spatula before inverting onto a platter. Serve warm with ice cream or custard. This dessert reheats very well in the microwave, and can be made a few days ahead. Can be frozen. Defrost before warming.

SERVES 8-10

GRILLED FRESH FRUIT SERVED WITH GINGER MASCARPONE

STEAMED CHOCOLATE PUDDING

GRILLED FIGS AND NECTARINES WITH VANILLA CUSTARD

This has to be one of the easiest and most impressive desserts you will ever make. It can be assembled at the last minute and looks spectacular.

6 FRESH FIGS, CUT IN HALF
6 NECTARINES or PEACHES, CUT IN HALF, PIP REMOVED*
TREACLE BROWN SUGAR

Place cut fruit on an ovenproof serving platter, cut side up. Just before serving cover the cut side tightly with brown sugar covering complete surface.

Preheat the grill.

Place fruit directly under the grill and watch carefully while the sugar sizzles and caramelises. Remove from oven after 5 minutes.

Serve with Vanilla Custard or ice cream.

VANILLA CUSTARD
250ml (1 cup) vanilla yoghurt
250ml (1 cup) ready-made custard

Whisk the two ingredients together. Pour into a serving jug.

* Canned peach halves can be substituted if drained and dried very well. Grill exactly as for fresh fruit.

SERVES 6-8

FRESH FRUIT IN REDUCED JUICE

A refreshing fruit dessert flavoured with the strong juice.

750ml (3 cups) FRESH MANGO or TROPICAL JUICE
45ml (3 Tbs) HONEY
5ml (1 tsp) VANILLA ESSENCE

6 NECTARINES, UNPEELED AND CUT IN HALF
6 PEACHES, UNPEELED AND CUT IN HALF

Heat juice in a pot, bring to a boil and simmer until reduced and you have 2 cups of liquid. Stir in the honey and vanilla essence.

Add cut up fruit. Simmer for 5 minutes. Remove from stove and cool before refrigerating.

NOTE: Any seasonal fruit, such as apples, pears, pineapple can be used when nectarines and peaches are out of season. This dessert is best made and served the day you need it as the fruit discolours if cut too far in advance.

SERVES 8-10

GRILLED FIGS AND NECTARINES WITH VANILLA CUSTARD

FRESH FRUIT IN REDUCED JUICE

BERRY TIRAMISU FILLED PAVLOVA

This makes such a colourful, fresh variation of the usual tiramisu, and has meringue as a bonus.

PAVLOVA

4 EGG WHITES
250ml (1 cup) SUGAR

Preheat oven to 110°C (225°F).

Beat egg whites in a mixmaster with wire whisk until stiff. Add sugar, a tablespoonful at a time over 20 minutes until all sugar is mixed in. Shape meringue into a shell onto a baking tray lined with sprayed baking paper or onto an exopat mat.*

Bake for 1 hour. Turn oven off and leave in oven until meringue has dried out. If making ahead, keep meringue well sealed in an airtight container until ready to use.

BERRY TIRAMISU
3 EGGS, SEPARATED
250ml (1 cup) MASCARPONE
80ml (1/3 cup) CASTOR SUGAR
250ml (1 cup) CREAM, WHIPPED
200g (7 oz) FINGER BISCUITS or SAVOIARDI BISCUITS
375ml (1 1/2 cups) ORANGE or GRAPE JUICE
30ml (2 Tbs) COINTREAU or
OTHER ORANGE LIQUEUR
500g (16 oz) FROZEN or FRESH MIXED BERRIES
250g (8 oz) STRAWBERRIES

Whip cream in mixmaster until stiff. Set aside.
In the same bowl, beat egg yolks with sugar until thick and creamy. Add mascarpone and continue to beat until stiffened. Set aside.
In a clean bowl, beat egg whites until stiff. Fold into egg yolk mixture.

Fold whipped cream and egg/mascarpone mixture together gently. Then fold in the berries (not strawberries), leaving some for decoration. (If using frozen berries, do not defrost them).

Mix orange/grape juice and Cointreau together. Dip biscuits lightly into this mixture. They should not be too soggy. Place them in an open pyrex dish in a layer beside one another. Spoon half the berry mixture on top. Layer with more biscuits and finish with remaining berry mixture. Place in the fridge to set. (This can be done the day before).

TO SERVE: Scoop large squares with a lifter, placing them at different angles into the pavlova shell 1-2 hours before serving. Decorate with more berries and strawberries. Refrigerate until ready to use.

NOTE: The pavlova can be made a few days before. The tiramisu keeps well overnight in the fridge.

* See appendix

SERVES 10-12

BANANA SPLIT STRUDEL

If you have ever really enjoyed a banana split, imagine it in a pastry!

375ml (1 1/2 cups) RICOTTA CHEESE
80ml (1/3 cup) SMOOTH FIRM CREAM CHEESE
125ml (1/2 cup) SUGAR
1 EGG YOLK
15ml (1 Tbs) FLOUR
VANILLA ESSENCE

3-4 BANANAS, SLICED THICKLY AT AN ANGLE

100g (3 oz) GRATED DARK CHOCOLATE

5 SHEETS PHYLLO

62g (4 Tbs) MELTED UNSALTED BUTTER FOR BRUSHING

Preheat oven to 180°C (375°F). Place baking paper or an exopat mat on a large baking tray. Set aside.

Brush each of 5 sheets of phyllo with melted butter, sprinkling a little chocolate between alternate layers.

Mix ricotta cheese, cream cheese, sugar, egg yolk, vanilla and flour together. Stir in sliced bananas. Spread mixture down long side of phyllo. Roll up to enclose filling, pinching ends together. Brush outside with butter and sprinkle with more chocolate.

Place strudel on the prepared tray. Bake for 30 minutes or until golden. Serve warm.

NOTE: The strudel can be prepared earlier in the day, covered with plastic wrap and placed unbaked on the baking tray in the fridge. Uncover and bring to room temperature before baking. It can also be reheated on a 140°C (325°F) oven if already baked.

SERVES 10-12

BERRY TIRAMISU FILLED PAVLOVA

CRÈME CARAMEL

This is undoubtedly the best crème caramel you will ever make. It was handed down to me by my mother, and will be one you will make again and again.

500ml (2 cups) MILK
250ml (1 cup) CREAM
250ml (1 cup) THICK CREAM
175ml ($^{3}/_{4}$ cup) CASTOR SUGAR
5ml (1 tsp) VANILLA

6 JUMBO EGGS
2 EGG YOLKS

CARAMEL
250ml (1 cup) SUGAR
30ml (2 Tbs) COLD WATER

Preheat oven to 160°C (350°F).

Prepare caramel: Place sugar and water in frying pan over high heat. Do not stir. Swirl pan only if necessary. Sugar will melt, crystallize and re-melt. When it starts to brown watch it carefully. Pour into a long 30cm (12 inch) loaf tin. Allow to cool and set.

Heat milk, cream, castor sugar and vanilla gently in a pot. Whisk to remove lumps. Beat eggs and egg yolks very slowly with a hand beater or whisk. Stir egg mixture into milk mixture VERY SLOWLY through a strainer. Pour onto caramel in loaf tin. Cover well with foil and seal sides.

Pour boiling water into a roasting pan and immerse the loaf tin into the water to come halfway up the sides of the loaf tin.

Place on middle rack of oven and immediately turn temp. down to 140°C (325°F). Bake for 70 mins. Bake another 10 mins or more if not set.

Remove from oven. Cool covered with foil. Refrigerate overnight.

TO UNMOULD: Place tin in hot water for a few seconds. Invert crème caramel onto platter, and then re-dip outside of tin base into boiling water to loosen remaining caramel to drizzle over.

NOTE: It is important to check the crème caramel after 40 minutes to see that there are no bubbles. (If the oven is too hot, the caramel will have bubbles running through it). Should it not be completely set after the baking time, leave it in the oven a little longer. It will set in the refrigerator.

SERVES 10-12

BANANA TARTE TATIN

A stunning variation on the apple theme.

6 FIRM, RIPE BANANAS
200g (7 oz) ROLL PUFF PASTRY

375ml (1 $^{1}/_{2}$ cups) SUGAR
45ml (3 Tbs) WATER
175ml ($^{3}/_{4}$ cup) CREAM

1 EGG LIGHTLY BEATEN WITH A LITTLE WATER

Melt sugar and water over medium-high heat until melted and caramelised.

Heat cream gently. Stir into caramel mixture.

Lightly grease or spray a 24 cm (9 inch) pie dish or individual tart dishes. Spoon a little sauce into each dish.

Slice bananas thickly at an angle and place like a fan on top of the caramel sauce.

Roll out puff pastry and place on top of bananas, tucked into the sides of the dish. Brush with a little beaten egg.

Bake in a preheated oven 200°C (400°F) for 15-20 mins or until golden.

Run a knife around the edges of the dish. Place a plate or platter on top of dish and invert the tatin. Serve immediately with ice cream or cream.

SERVES 6

BANANA TARTE TATIN

PLUM TART

A crisp pastry encloses tangy plums to make this an easy-to-make, gorgeous free-form tart. Other fresh fruits such as peaches or apricots can be substituted. The fruit should not ooze too much juice when baking.

PASTRY
250ml (1 cup) FLOUR
5ml (1 tsp) SUGAR
2.5ml (1/2 tsp) BAKING POWDER
2.5ml (1/2 tsp) SALT
62.5g (4 Tbs) COLD UNSALTED BUTTER
45ml (3 Tbs) SOUR CREAM/CREAM CHEESE

Combine flour, sugar, baking powder and salt in a food processor. Add cut up butter and process until mixture resembles fine breadcrumbs. Add sour cream or cream cheese and process until mixture just starts to form a ball.
Place in plastic wrap, shaped into a flat disc and refrigerate for at least 30 minutes before using.

FILLING
750g (1 1/2 lbs) FRESH RED PLUMS
60ml (1/4 cup) SUGAR
30ml (2 Tbs) FLOUR
30ml (2 Tbs) ICING SUGAR
1 EGG BEATEN WITH WATER

Preheat oven to 200°C (400°F).
Peel plums, halve and remove pip. Toss with the sugar in a bowl. Set aside.

Roll out dough onto a floured surface into a 34 cm (15 inch) round. Place dough on baking tray lined with baking paper or on an exopat mat. *
Sprinkle with flour. Place plums, cut side up on flour, leaving a 3cm (1 inch) border all around. Sprinkle them with icing sugar.

Fold edges of dough to enclose the plums.
Brush outer edges with lightly beaten egg.
Bake about 20-30 minutes or until golden. Cool for about 10 mins before serving.

NOTE: This dessert can be served at room temperature. It does not need to be served warm. Ice cream, custard or cream complement the tartness of the fruit. It should be baked and served on the day you are using it for maximum freshness.

* See appendix

SERVES 6-8

FRUITY ICE CREAM PARFAIT

Everybody loves a refreshing, fruity ice cream and this one looks spectacular with its 3 different layers.

12 FRESH GRANADILLAS, PULPED
250ml (1 cup) CREAM or NON-DAIRY CREAM*
3 JUMBO EGGS
175ml (3/4 cup) CASTOR SUGAR

In a mixmaster, beat cream or non-dairy cream until stiff. Add eggs, sugar and granadilla pulp and mix together. Place in a glass bowl or loaf tin and set in freezer. (Stir after a few hours, because granadillas sink to the bottom).

500g (16 oz) RASPBERRIES, STRAWBERRIES or MIXED BERRIES (FRESH OR FROZEN)

SUGAR SYRUP
125ml (1/2 cup) SUGAR
125ml (1/2 cup) WATER

Boil sugar and water together for a few minutes until syrupy. Then cool.

Process berries in food processor. Add sugar syrup and pour on top of granadilla ice cream. Place in freezer to set.

3 FRESH MANGOES, PURÉED or 500ml (2 cups) MANGO PURÉE (FROM CANS)
250ml (1 cup) CREAM or NON-DAIRY CREAM
3 JUMBO EGGS
175ml (3/4 cup) CASTOR SUGAR

In a mixmaster, beat cream or non-dairy cream until stiff. Add eggs, sugar and mango pulp and mix together. Set on top of berry mixture in freezer.

NOTE: This dessert must be made several days before required in order to set each layer. Remove ice cream from freezer about 15 minutes before serving to soften.

* See appendix

SERVES 10-12

PLUM TART

FLOATING ISLAND

This is so light it is like eating air, with a sweet vanilla sauce as its base.

4 EGG WHITES
175ml ($^3/_4$ cup) SUGAR
DROP OF VANILLA ESSENCE

Preheat oven to 140°C (325°F).

Beat egg whites until stiff. Add sugar very slowly over 20 minutes until meringue is thick.

Line a loaf tin 25cm (10 inch) with wax paper on the bottom. Spray with non-stick cooking spray.

Spoon in the meringue mixture. Place a piece of wax paper on top.

Place loaf tin in a bain-marie* so that water comes halfway up the sides of the tin. Bake for 50-60 minutes. Turn oven off and cool in oven for 20-30 minutes. Remove meringue from oven and peel off top piece of wax paper. Invert tin onto a platter, carefully remove it and then 2nd piece of wax paper from meringue.

* bain-marie - a roasting pan filled 2cm (1 inch) deep with boiling water in which you place another baking tin in order to bake on a more gentle heat in the oven.

CRÈME ANGLAISE
2 EGG YOLKS
30ml (2 Tbs) CASTOR SUGAR
5ml (1 tsp) VANILLA ESSENCE or EXTRACT
500ml (2 cups) MILK **

Beat egg yolks with sugar until very thick and creamy. Add vanilla.

Heat milk in a heavy-bottomed pot. Add beaten egg mixture and allow to thicken slightly. Do not bring to a boil. Cool until ready to use.

Spoon sauce around the base of the floating island just before serving.

Note: Ensure that the meringue is semi-cool before removing from the oven or it will drop in volume with the sudden change in temperature. The crème anglaise can be made 2 days ahead and refrigerated. It can be made using Rich's Whip Kream Base **(see appendix) if you require a non-dairy dessert.

SERVES 6-8

SHAVED MANGO TART

This is one of those "wow" desserts, which will make you look like a genius. It tastes as sensational as it looks, and you can pretend that you stood for hours making it! Experiment with other fresh seasonal fruits, but be careful of ones that change colour when cut.

200g (7 oz) ROLL PUFF PASTRY
1 EGG BEATEN
2-3 LARGE RIPE, FIBRELESS MANGOES
30ml (2 Tbs) LIME RIND

Preheat oven to 200°C (400°F).

Roll out puff pastry onto a floured surface into a large rectangle. Brush entire edge of the dough with a little beaten egg. Cut flat strips from excess pastry and build up a 2 cm (1 inch) border along the edge of the dough, which will become a baked base to enclose the filling. Secure the corners with toothpicks to ensure that the dough does not collapse on the sides whilst baking.

Prick the entire base with a fork. Place on an exopat mat or baking paper on a baking tray. Brush base with beaten egg and bake for 15-20 minutes or until pastry is golden. Allow to cool before filling.

FILLING
375ml (1 $^1/_2$ cups) RICOTTA CHEESE
60ml ($^1/_4$ cup) CASTOR SUGAR
60ml ($^1/_4$ cup) MILK or CREAM
5ml (1 tsp) VANILLA ESSENCE

Place ricotta, castor sugar, milk or cream and vanilla essence in food processor and process until smooth. Spread over centre of pre-baked base.

Using a mandolin or very sharp vegetable peeler, shave slices of mango and arrange in curls attractively on top of the filling. Sprinkle with a little additional castor sugar and decorate with lime rind.

NOTE: Base can be made a few days ahead and kept sealed in plastic wrap. Filling can be prepared up to 2 days ahead. Only fill a few hours before serving.

SERVES 8-10

FLOATING ISLAND

SHAVED MANGO TART

LEMON, LIME AND LEMONGRASS ICE CREAM

This is one of the creamiest ice creams you will ever make. It is a taste sensation which melts in your mouth with its different textures. The secret is in the beating of the mixture over the double boiler, which forms the creamy base of the ice cream.

60ml ($^1/_4$ cup) FRESH LEMON JUICE
60ml ($^1/_4$ cup) FRESH LIME JUICE
15ml (1 Tbs) FRESH LEMON RIND
15ml (1 Tbs) LIME RIND
30ml (2 Tbs) LEMONGRASS, VERY FINELY CHOPPED*
4 EGGS, SEPARATED
250ml (1 cup) SUGAR
125ml ($^1/_2$ cup) CONDENSED MILK
250ml (1 cup) CREAM

Place lemon juice, lime juice, both rinds, lemongrass, egg yolks and sugar in a double boiler over medium heat. Beat with an electric hand beater or whisk until very pale, yellow and thickened (this may take 20 mins). The thicker you beat it the better the consistency of the ice cream.

Remove from stove and stir in condensed milk. Allow to cool slightly.

Beat egg whites very stiffly in the mixmaster on high. Turn the machine down to a lower speed and slowly pour the yolk and juice mixture into the whites to blend. (This cools the egg mixture and maintains the smooth texture of the beaten egg white).

In a separate bowl, beat the cream until stiff.

Fold egg mixture into cream and pour into a loaf tin or a glass bowl. Set overnight in freezer.

NOTE: This can be made well ahead of time and kept in the freezer. Defrost for about 15 minutes before serving to soften the ice cream.

* Always remove the tough outer leaves. Chop very finely. Use only the base of the lemongrass stem when cooking.

SERVES 8-10

PISTACHIO ICE CREAM

A sensational, different ice cream, which is so easy to make.

500ml (2 cups) CREAM or NON-DAIRY CREAM
4 EGGS
10ml (2 tsps) VANILLA ESSENCE or SEEDS OF 1 VANILLA BEAN
80ml ($^1/_3$ cup) CASTOR SUGAR
250ml (1 cup) PEELED GREEN PISTACHIO NUTS, CHOPPED FINELY
250ml (1 cup) PEELED GREEN PISTACHIO NUTS (WHOLE)
DROPS OF GREEN FOOD COLOURING

Beat cream or non-dairy cream until very stiff. Add eggs and beat gently just to blend.

Add chopped and whole pistachios, vanilla and castor sugar. Stir to mix through.

Ice cream may require a few drops of green food colouring to enhance the colour.
Freeze in a glass bowl or loaf tin.

Remove from freezer 20 minutes before serving

Serve ice cream when soft and almost melting.

SERVES 8-10

LEMON, LIME AND LEMONGRASS ICE CREAM AND PISTACHIO ICE CREAM

BAKLAVA ICE CREAM LOAF

My family polish this dessert off and even lick the platter when I make it! The completed dessert is a sandwich of phyllo nut layers with ice cream in the middle. Once you have mastered this, it will be such a smash hit that you will make it again and again. The phyllo stays crispy even when frozen and makes a crunchy, sweet syrupy contrast to the ice cream.

8 SHEETS PHYLLO PASTRY
60ml (1/4 cup) MELTED BUTTER or MARGARINE

100g (3 oz) GROUND ALMONDS
100g (3 oz) EITHER NIBBED ALMONDS or CHOPPED PISTACHIOS
10ml (2 tsps) CINNAMON
10ml (2 tsps) CASTOR SUGAR

Mix the nuts, cinnamon and sugar together in a small bowl. Set aside.

2 litres (8 cups) VANILLA ICE CREAM (BOUGHT)

Preheat oven to 160°C (350°F).

Brush 2 sheets of phyllo with melted butter and place one on top of the other. Sprinkle with a third of the nut mixture. Repeat procedure twice placing all the phyllo sheets on top of one another. Brush the remaining 2 sheets of phyllo with butter and place on top. Cut in half vertically to make 2 long rectangles.

Cut a diamond pattern into the top of each rectangle with a sharp knife. Place the 2 rectangles on a baking tray. Bake until golden at least 30-45 minutes. Cool. (These form the top and bottom of the sandwich).

SYRUP
160ml (2/3 cup) SUGAR
160ml (2/3 cup) WATER
JUICE OF 1/2 LEMON

Mix sugar, water and lemon juice and boil gently for a few minutes until syrupy. Line a long loaf tin with foil (for easy removal).

Place 1 rectangle of baked phyllo in the loaf tin. Pour over half the syrup.

Cool. Soften ice cream and press down on top of phyllo and mould to the shape of the loaf tin. Place last rectangle on top of ice cream.

Pour remainder of syrup over this half of phyllo. Freeze until set.

Remove from freezer 20 minutes before serving to soften ice cream. Then remove from loaf tin.
Pull away the foil and place on a platter.

NOTE: This ice cream can be made and frozen long in advance.

SERVES 10-12

WATERMELON GRANITA

When the watermelon is as sweet as sugar, this is the most refreshing dessert, which is served like shaved ice.

1 litre (4 cups) WATERMELON, CHOPPED AND SEEDED
80ml (1/3 cup) SUGAR
175ml (3/4 cup) WATER
15-30ml (1-2 Tbs) LEMON JUICE

Bring water and sugar to a boil and boil for a few minutes. Add lemon juice.

Place watermelon in food processor and process until smooth.

Allow sugar syrup to cool. Add to processed watermelon.

Place mixture in a shallow flat tin and place in freezer to set. After a few hours, stir with a fork. Place back in freezer.

MAKES ± 1 1/2 LITRES (6 CUPS)

BAKLAVA ICE CREAM LOAF

MANGO SORBET

A wonderful, fruity and creamy sorbet.

750ml (3 cups) MANGO PURÉE (FROM 5 LARGE MANGOES)*
1 EGG WHITE

SUGAR SYRUP
250ml (1 cup) SUGAR
250ml (1 cup) WATER

Boil sugar and water on medium high heat until slightly thickened (for about 5 minutes). Set aside.

Liquidise mangoes in food processor. Add cooled sugar syrup. Stir in the unbeaten egg white.

Freeze the mixture. When purée is almost frozen, place the semi-frozen mixture into a food processor in batches and process in small quantities until smooth. Continue until you have processed all the mixture. It should now be light and fluffy.

Refreeze until ready to serve.

ICE CREAM MACHINE: Place entire mixture in machine after processing, adding sugar syrup and unbeaten egg white and churn until it makes a sorbet.

* When mangoes are out of season, drain 3 x 400g (14 oz) cans mango and liquidise the pulp.

MAKES 1 LITRE (4 CUPS)

PLUM SORBET

You will lick your lips because these plums make such a wonderful tasting sorbet.

1kg (2.2 lbs) PLUMS (RED)
325ml (1 ⅓ cups) TREACLE BROWN SUGAR
750ml (3 cups) WATER
10ml (2 tsps) VANILLA ESSENCE
RED FOOD COLOURING
30ml (2 Tbs) LEMON JUICE

Peel and cook plums in sugar, water and vanilla for 8-10 minutes.

Cool and then process in food processor until smooth. Adjust sugar and omit lemon juice (if plums are sour). Add food colouring to make sorbet redder.

Freeze in a shallow flat container. When frozen, stir with a fork to fluff. Process again until smooth (if desired).

Refreeze until ready to use. Serve slightly defrosted.

MAKES APPROX. 1 LITRE (4 CUPS)

FIG ICE CREAM

I love the combination of figs and ginger, which make a sensational dessert.

1 ½ litres (6 cups) VANILLA ICE CREAM
5 WHOLE PRESERVED FIGS
45ml (3 Tbs) FIG SYRUP
125ml (½ cup) PRESERVED GINGER PIECES
30ml (2 Tbs) GINGER SYRUP
150g (5 oz) DRIED FIGS
10ml (2 tsps) GROUND GINGER

Place dried figs in a little water, cover and heat in the microwave for 1-2 minutes to soften them. Drain and cool.

Place preserved figs, dried figs and preserved ginger in a food processor and process with metal blade until finely chopped.

Soften vanilla ice cream. Stir in mixture from food processor as well as ginger syrup, fig syrup and ground ginger. Mix well.

Set in a small loaf tin or a glass bowl until ready to use.

NOTE: When buying preserved figs and ginger, use the syrup in which they are bottled as your fig and ginger syrup.

SERVES 8-10

MANGO SORBET, PLUM SORBET AND WATERMELON GRANITA

WHITE CHOCOLATE CHEESECAKE

Baking

CHOCOLATE BISCOTTI

FLORENTINE TART

FLOURLESS ORANGE CAKE

PECAN SQUARES

Baking

Bakin

This section definitely rates as one of my most favourite because each recipe is more delicious and calorie-laden than the next. I don't count calories when I am baking, because I like to indulge in the simple pleasure of enjoying each mouthful. So, enjoy each and every one of these delicious recipes!

Remember that freshly baked cakes, muffins or biscuits are always much nicer than those that are reheated, but often it is not always possible to bake at the last minute, so I have indicated which recipes can be made ahead and which keep well.

One only needs to be precise in measurement when baking, so ensure that you have the correct measuring utensils. Always preheat your oven before preparing the ingredients, and bake on the middle rack to ensure even heat. An important tip to remember is that some ovens are hotter or cooler than others, and you should, therefore adjust your baking time accordingly - I call it "getting to know your oven".

I always use jumbo eggs as they are the best size for baking. An important tip to remember when baking muffins, is that one should never over mix the batter, nor bake on too low a temperature for best rising and texture results.

Baking

QUICK AND EASY

- CHOCOLATE MERINGUES
- FAT FREE APPLE PIE
- PISTACHIO CRISPS
- CHOCOLATE SPIRALS

RECIPES

- BLUEBERRY DANISH
- MIXED BERRY NUT MUFFINS
- WHITE CHOCOLATE CHEESECAKE
- CHOCOLATE BISCOTTI
- APPLE PHYLLO TRIANGLES
- APPLE JALOUSIE
- FLORENTINE TART
- PECAN AND JAM MUFFINS
- FLOURLESS ORANGE CAKE
- STICKY CINNAMON BUNS
- CHOCOLATE LOG WITH CHOCOLATE CREAM FILLING
- CARAMELISED LEMON TART
- CHUNKY CHOCOLATE CHIPPERS
- PECAN SQUARES
- SESAME CRISPS

CHOCOLATE MERINGUES

250ml (1 cup) SUGAR
4 EGG WHITES
30ml (2 Tbs) COCOA
125ml ($^1/_2$ cup) GRATED DARK CHOCOLATE

Preheat oven to 120°C (200°F).

Beat whites in mixmaster with a wire whisk until very stiff. Add 1 Tbs sugar at a time over 20 minutes to ensure that the whites absorb the sugar. Continue beating until all the sugar has been added.

Lastly fold in the cocoa and grated chocolate and mix lightly to blend.

Drop spoonfuls or pipe meringues onto a baking tray lined with baking paper or with an exopat mat.

Bake for 40 minutes. Turn oven off and leave in oven to dry out for a few more hours.
Store in Tupperware.

MAKES 20

FAT FREE APPLE PIE

385g (13 oz) CAN PIE APPLES
45ml (3 Tbs) TREACLE BROWN SUGAR

BATTER
1 EGG, BEATEN
125ml ($^1/_2$ cup) SUGAR
125ml ($^1/_2$ cup) FLOUR
125ml ($^1/_2$ cup) APPLE SAUCE
5ml (1 tsp) BAKING POWDER
5ml (1 tsp) VANILLA ESSENCE

Preheat oven to 180°C (375°F).

Pre-spray a 24cm (9 inch) pie dish. Place apples at bottom of pie dish. Sprinkle with a little brown sugar.

Mix all ingredients for batter together. Pour over apples. Bake for 35-40 mins or until golden.

SERVES 6-8

PISTACHIO CRISPS

2 EGG WHITES
160ml ($^2/_3$ cup) CASTOR SUGAR
100g ($3^1/_2$ oz) SHELLED PISTACHIOS (or PECANS)

RICE PAPER SHEETS

Preheat oven to 190°C (380°F).

Line a baking tray with the rice paper sheets.
Beat egg whites until very stiff. Add the castor sugar and continue beating for a few more minutes. Crush nuts in food processor until very fine. Fold them into whites. Drop spoonfuls onto rice paper and flatten them a little. Bake for 8-10 mins or until set and lightly golden.

Cool slightly and then keep in a Tupperware.

MAKES ± 20-25

CHOCOLATE SPIRALS

200g (7 oz) PUFF PASTRY
POPPY SEEDS
CASTOR SUGAR
MILK OR EGG FOR BRUSHING
1 BOTTLE CHOCOLATE-HAZELNUT SPREAD*

Preheat oven to 190°C (380°F).

Unroll puff pastry. Do not roll out more. Spread with chocolate-hazelnut spread. Sprinkle with castor sugar, and then generously with poppy seeds. Roll up again, dampening edge with a little milk to seal. Brush entire outside of roll with milk or egg. Place roll in fridge for $^1/_2$ hour before baking.

Cut into 12-14 circles. Turn and lay flat on baking paper or exopat mat on a baking tray. Sprinkle with additional castor sugar. Bake for 10 mins.

* Nutella or Pralinutta

MAKES ± 20

BLUEBERRY DANISH

BLUEBERRY DANISH

A steaming cup of coffee accompanies this Danish perfectly to make a quick and easy-to-make bake.

DOUGH

500ml (2 cups) FLOUR
10ml (2 tsps) BAKING POWDER
2.5ml (1/2 tsp) SALT
175ml (3/4 cup) LOW FAT CHUNKY COTTAGE CHEESE
80ml (1/3 cup) SUGAR
60ml (1/4 cup) MILK
60ml (1/4 cup) OIL
1 EGG
5ml (1 tsp) VANILLA ESSENCE

Mix together the flour, baking powder and salt. Set aside.

In a food processor, process cottage cheese until smooth. Add sugar, milk, oil, egg and vanilla and process until smooth.

Add flour mixture and pulse to mix in until dough becomes sticky. Gently knead a little on a floured surface and shape into a disk. Place it in plastic wrap in the fridge for at least 1/2 hour.

FILLING

125ml (1/2 cup) LOW FAT SMOOTH COTTAGE CHEESE
60ml (1/4 cup) SUGAR
1 EGG YOLK
10ml (2 tsps) LEMON RIND
5ml (1 tsp) VANILLA ESSENCE
250ml (1 cup) FRESH BLUEBERRIES (OR CANNED, WELL DRAINED)
1 EGG BEATEN WITH WATER (FOR BRUSHING)

In a food processor, process cottage cheese with sugar until creamy. Add egg yolk, lemon rind and vanilla.

Preheat oven to 200°C (400°F). Place sprayed baking paper on a baking tray.

Roll out the dough into a large rectangle and then transfer onto the baking paper. Spread cream cheese mixture down the centre of dough, leaving space on sides. Sprinkle blueberries over cream cheese mixture.

Make 3 cm (1 inch) cuts along each side of the dough at an angle, trimming off corners. Plait strips over each other.

In a small bowl, beat egg with a little water and brush over pastry. Bake for 20-25 minutes or until golden. Allow to cool slightly.

GLAZE

125ml (1/2 cup) ICING SUGAR
30-45ml (2-3 Tbs) LEMON JUICE

Mix icing sugar and lemon juice together until smooth. Drizzle glaze over Danish.

SERVES 10-12

MIXED BERRY NUT MUFFINS

So quick and easy and filled with colourful berries and nuts, these are always a hit.

30g (2 Tbs) UNSALTED BUTTER
125ml (1/2 cup) SUGAR
2 EGGS
675ml (2 3/4 cups) FLOUR
7.5ml (1 1/2 tsps) BAKING POWDER
2.5ml (1/2 tsp) BICARBONATE OF SODA
375ml (1 1/2 cups) SOUR CREAM
5ml (1 tsp) VANILLA ESSENCE

625ml (1 1/2 cups) MIXED FRESH or FROZEN BERRIES
100g (3 oz) SLIVERED ALMONDS, TOASTED

Toast slivered almonds on a baking tray on 140°C (300°F) for 10 mins.

Preheat oven to 180°C (375°F).

Beat softened butter with sugar until fluffy. Add eggs, one at a time. Then fold in sour cream and lastly dry ingredients and vanilla. Do not over mix.

Toss berries lightly with a little sugar. Then mix into dough. Place spoonfuls into sprayed muffin tins until quite full. Top with toasted almonds.

Bake for 20-25 mins or until golden. Allow to cool before removing from tin.

MAKES 10 OR 6 GIANT MUFFINS

MIXED BERRY NUT MUFFINS

WHITE CHOCOLATE CHEESECAKE

I am known for decadent cheesecakes, but this one tops them all with the white chocolate marble. Enjoy each rich slice, because there will definitely not be any leftovers.

CRUST
250g (8 oz) CHOCOLATE BISCUITS
60ml (4 Tbs) MELTED BUTTER

Preheat oven to 160°C (350°F).
Crush biscuits in food processor until very finely crushed. Add melted butter.
Spread onto base & 1/4 way up sides of a 24cm (9 inch) springform tin.
Bake for 5-10 mins. Remove and cool for 10 mins.
Turn oven down to 140°C (300°F).

FILLING
500ml (2 cups) CREAM CHEESE (FULL CREAM)
250ml (1 cup) MASCARPONE
250ml (1 cup) SOUR CREAM
80ml (1/3 cup) FLOUR

3 EGGS BEATEN
175ml (3/4 cup) CASTOR SUGAR

300g (9 oz) WHITE CHOCOLATE, MELTED
80ml (1/3 cup) MILK, WARMED
1 EGG YOLK

In a mixmaster, lightly beat the cream cheese, mascarpone, sour cream and flour until smooth.
In a separate bowl, beat the eggs and sugar.
Add to cream cheese mixture and beat until blended.

Meanwhile, melt white chocolate in microwave or in a double boiler. Do not allow to burn. Cool slightly and then whisk in the warm milk and then egg yolk until smooth.

Pour half of the cheese mixture into prepared tin. Then pour in some white chocolate mixture. Pour in remaining cheese mixture and more of the white chocolate on top. Marble with a knife or spatula.

Bake for 1 hour. Turn oven off and leave in for a further 40 mins to cool.

TOPPING
250ml (1 cup) SOUR CREAM
80ml (1/3 cup) CASTOR SUGAR

GRATED CHOCOLATE or BERRIES

Remove from oven and spread with topping. Serve at room temperature. Do not refrigerate as cheesecake texture should be soft but not firm.

NOTE: Unlike other cheesecakes which are refrigerated to firm them, this one tastes better when it is cooled, but not refrigerated. Can be made in the morning and left out all day, it will be fine.

SERVES 12

CHOCOLATE BISCOTTI

Crunchy and crispy these make a delicious change from the usual biscotti. Dipped into melted chocolate, they become a chocolate lover's dream.

160ml (2/3 cup) WHOLE BLANCHED ALMONDS

175ml (3/4 cup) FLOUR
100g (3 oz) DARK or MILK CHOCOLATE GRATED
125ml (1/2 cup) SUGAR
60ml (1/4 cup) COCOA POWDER

2 EGGS, BEATEN
5ml (1 tsp) VANILLA ESSENCE
1 EGG WHITE

Preheat oven to 160°C (350°F).

Place nuts on a baking tray and toast for 10 minutes in the oven. Allow to cool.

Line a large baking tray with baking paper or an exopat mat.

Combine flour, chocolate, sugar and cocoa powder. Add beaten eggs and vanilla and mix to form a stiff dough. Dough will be slightly sticky. Dust hands with flour and shape into 3 wide logs and place on baking paper or mat.

Brush with beaten egg white. Bake for 30 minutes.

Remove from oven, turn down oven temperature to 140°C (300°F) and slice on a slight diagonal into thick slices. Place back on baking tray, sliced side up and bake again for another 20 minutes or until dried out.

NOTE: These keep very well in Tupperware, or can be frozen. Ends can be dipped into melted chocolate for decoration.

MAKES ± 24

CHOCOLATE BISCOTTI

APPLE PHYLLO TRIANGLES

You will get rave reviews when you make these, and they look awesome on a platter. Once you get the hang of making them, they are really quite simple, so the next time they'll be a breeze. Just make extra in case you eat too many as you are baking.

16 SHEETS OF PHYLLO
10 RED APPLES, UNPEELED, CORED AND THINLY SLICED IN WHOLE SLICES
125g (8 Tbs) MELTED MARGARINE or BUTTER FOR BRUSHING
ICING SUGAR FOR DUSTING

Preheat oven to 200°C (400°F).

Brush each of 8 sheets of phyllo with margarine or butter.

Cut 5 apples into paper-thin rounds with a mandoline or very sharp knife. Cover phyllo with apple slices in rows running down the length of the phyllo. Brush them with more margarine or butter and dust them generously with icing sugar.

First cut the phyllo with a very sharp knife in rows vertically between the apple rounds. Then cut horizontally along the phyllo dividing the apples into 4 rows. Next make diagonal cuts from corner to corner in each rectangle, giving you long triangles. Place them onto sprayed baking paper or an exopat mat on a baking tray.

Bake for 10-15 minutes or until golden and crisp on the underneath side. (The outer edges of the baking tray will brown first). Remove and place on a rack to cool.

Repeat with remaining other 8 sheets and other 5 apples as above.

Dust with more icing sugar before serving and pile them on top of a platter to serve.

NOTE: These can be made ahead, but should not be covered except with paper towel, or they will go soggy. They can be recrisped by placing them back into a medium oven and heated gently.

MAKES 36

APPLE JALOUSIE

The taste of a dried apple is much stronger than that of a fresh one, which then enhances the flavour of this wonderfully easy and different apple strudel.

250g (8 oz) DRIED APPLES
125ml (1/2 cup) CASTOR SUGAR
5ml (1 tsp) CINNAMON

200g (7 oz) PUFF PASTRY

1 EGG WITH A LITTLE WATER FOR BRUSHING
ICING SUGAR FOR DUSTING

Preheat oven 200°C (400°F).

Place apples in a pot and cover with water. Bring to a boil and simmer until soft. Allow to cool. Drain. Coarsely chop in food processor with castor sugar and cinnamon.

Roll out puff pastry into a rectangle. Cut lengthwise in half. Place 1 half on sprayed baking paper or exopat mat on a baking tray.

Brush pastry with beaten egg. Spread apple mixture down the centre of puff pastry, leaving a border along edges. Top with other half of pastry and cut deep slashes all the way down the sides.
Seal edges with your fingers.

Bake for 15-20 mins or until golden. Allow to cool and dust with icing sugar. Serve with whipped cream.

SERVES 8-10

APPLE PHY_LO TRIANGLES

FLORENTINE TART

This makes a gorgeous-looking nutty tart with a caramel glaze and changes the more common Florentine biscuit into a baker's delight.

185g (12 Tbs) BUTTER
125ml (½ cup) CASTOR SUGAR
1 EGG
15ml (1 Tbs) OIL
625ml (2½ cups) FLOUR
5ml (1 tsp) BAKING POWDER
2.5ml (½ tsp) SALT

150g (5 oz) DARK CHOCOLATE MELTED WITH
45ml (3 Tbs) MILK

Preheat oven to 180°C (375°F).

In food processor, cream butter and sugar. Add egg and oil, continuing to process. Add dry ingredients and process until dough forms. Press into bottom and up sides of 24cm (9 inch) loose-bottom tart tin or rectangular 25cm (10 inch) loaf tin. Prick all over with a fork. Bake base for 10-15 mins.

Remove from oven and spread with melted chocolate mixture. Cool slightly.

TOPPING
375ml (1½ cups) TREACLE BROWN SUGAR
160ml (⅔ cup) MILK
185g (12 Tbs) BUTTER
500g (16 oz) GLACE FRUIT MIX
250g (8 oz) RED GLACE CHERRIES
100g (3½ oz) WHOLE BLANCHED ALMONDS
100g (3½ oz) FLAKED ALMONDS
200g (7 oz) HAZELNUTS, WHOLE

Boil sugar, butter and milk for topping. Add remaining ingredients and stir until well coated. Pour over top of pre-baked tart base. Place tart back in oven for a further 10-15 mins. Remove and allow to cool.

NOTE: This can be made 1-2 days ahead and simply covered with plastic wrap until ready to use.

SERVES 8-10

PECAN AND JAM MUFFINS

A quick and easy delicious accompaniment to tea.

375ml (1½ cups) FLOUR
160ml (⅔ cup) TREACLE BROWN SUGAR
10ml (2 tsps) BAKING POWDER
2.5ml (½ tsp) SALT
PINCH OF NUTMEG
PINCH OF CINNAMON
60ml (¼ cup) OIL
160ml (⅔ cup) MILK
1 EGG

175ml (¾ cup) PECANS, CHOPPED

SMOOTH APRICOT JAM

Preheat oven to 200°C (400°F).

Spray a muffin tin with non-stick cooking spray.

Combine flour, sugar, baking powder, salt and spices.

Mix together the oil, milk and egg and add to dry ingredients. Stir in nuts. Do not over mix, just combine ingredients.

Spoon mixture ¾ full into muffins tins. Drop a teaspoonful of jam into the centre and make a slight indentation with a spoon. Bake for 20 mins.

NOTE: These are best made and served the day you eat them. Be careful not to put too much jam in the centre, or the jam will ooze and stick to the muffin tins.

MAKES 9-10 MUFFINS

FLORENTINE TART

FLOURLESS ORANGE CAKE

A wonderful, nutty moist cake, which has no oil, butter or flour. The polenta gives a nice change in the texture. Lemons can be exchanged for the oranges as a change of pace.

2 LARGE ORANGES OR 3 SMALL ORANGES

125g (4 oz) SHELLED PISTACHIOS
125g (4 oz) NIBBED or FLAKED ALMONDS
250ml (1 cup) CASTOR SUGAR
5ml (1 tsp) BAKING POWDER
125ml (½ cup) POLENTA
6 JUMBO EGGS

Preheat oven to 180°C (375°F).

Wash oranges and place them whole in a pot of water. Bring to a boil and boil for 2 hours or until softened. They must be soft. Allow to cool. Chop in food processor with skin. Remove all pips.

Place pistachios, almonds, castor sugar and polenta in food processor and process until quite fine. Add baking powder.

Beat eggs in mixmaster until very light and fluffy. Fold in nut mixture and oranges.

Line the bottom of a 24cm (9 inch) springform tin with baking paper. Spray with non-stick cooking spray. Pour mixture into tin. Bake 40-50 minutes or until golden.

SYRUP
250ml (1 cup) FRESH ORANGE JUICE
60ml (¼ cup) SYRUP

Heat orange juice and syrup in a pot. Bring to a boil and simmer without lid for 10 minutes until syrupy. Cool and pour over cake as it comes out of the oven.

NOTE: This cake freezes beautifully. Defrost overnight before serving. Alternatively, it can be made 1-2 days before serving.

SERVES 8-10

STICKY CINNAMON BUNS

You will adore these absolutely yummy sticky buns!

DOUGH
560ml (2¼ cups) FLOUR
80ml (⅓ cup) SUGAR
2.5ml (½ tsp) SALT
10g (½ oz) INSTANT DRY YEAST
160ml (⅔ cup) WARM WATER
30ml (2 Tbs) OIL
1 EGG

15ml (1 Tbs) CINNAMON
60ml (¼ cup) SUGAR

125ml (½ cup) CHOPPED PECANS

Preheat oven to 180°C (375°F). Line bottom of a 24cm (9 inch) springform tin with baking paper and spray with non-stick cooking spray. Place tin on a baking tray to avoid leaking in the oven.

In a large mixing bowl, mix dry ingredients together. Add warm water, oil and lightly beaten egg. Knead well until dough is smooth, adding additional flour as needed, making a soft pliable dough.

Place dough in a lightly oiled bowl covered with plastic wrap for about 1 hour to rise, or until it is soft and spongy.

Using a rolling pin, roll out onto a floured surface and sprinkle with sugar and cinnamon. Roll up like a Swiss roll. Cut into 7 very thick slices. Pour ½ of the sauce into prepared tin. Sprinkle sauce with ½ of the pecans. Place dough slices cut side up in a circle in the centre of the tin, leaving the outside edge unfilled. Drizzle with remaining sauce and pecans.
Bake for 40 minutes or until golden.

SAUCE
175ml (¾ cup) TREACLE BROWN SUGAR
80ml (⅓ cup) UNSALTED BUTTER
30ml (2 Tbs) SYRUP
60ml (¼ cup) WATER

Heat all ingredients in a small pot and simmer until sugar is dissolved. Set aside until ready to use.

Leave in tin for 10 mins to cool, and then pull buns apart and invert onto a platter with sauce on top. Allow to cool.

MAKES 7

FLOURLESS ORANGE CAKE

CHOCOLATE LOG WITH CHOCOLATE CREAM FILLING

When you want a decadent chocolate, calorie-laden cake, this light base filled with cream is the answer to your dreams!

180g (6 oz) DARK COOKING CHOCOLATE*
45ml (3 Tbs) WATER

Melt chocolate with water on high power in microwave for 30-40 seconds. Heat again for a further 40 seconds and whisk until chocolate is melted.

6 EGGS, SEPARATED
160ml (2/3 cup) SUGAR
PINCH OF SALT

15ml (1 Tbs) ICING SUGAR, SIFTED

Preheat oven to 160°C (350°F).

Line a large baking tray with baking paper and spray well.

Beat egg yolks with 80ml (1/3 cup) sugar and a pinch of salt until very creamy. Fold in melted chocolate and beat again until thickened. Set aside.

Beat egg whites until stiff and add remaining 80ml (1/3 cup) sugar. Beat a little longer.

Fold the two mixtures together. Spread into prepared tray.

Bake for 15-20 minutes until just set. Remove from oven and dust with icing sugar. Roll immediately in a clean cloth. Set aside to cool.

FILLING
250ml (1 cup) CREAM
80ml (1/3 cup) ICING SUGAR
125ml (1/2 cup) GRATED DARK CHOCOLATE
30ml (2 Tbs) GRAND MARNIER

Beat cream until stiff with icing sugar. Fold in grated chocolate and Grand Marnier.

Remove dishcloth. Spread cream on inside of chocolate log and roll up again and refrigerate until ready to serve. Dust outside with icing sugar and serve with strawberries or mixed berries if desired.

* If possible, use a good quality dark chocolate with a high cocoa butter content.

SERVES 10

CARAMELISED LEMON TART

If you like lemon, this is a delicious tart almost like the real-French version.

PASTRY
330ml (1 1/3 cups) FLOUR
45ml (3 Tbs) CASTOR SUGAR
10ml (2 tsps) LEMON RIND
PINCH SALT
125g (8 Tbs) UNSALTED BUTTER
30ml (2 Tbs) ICE WATER

In food processor, mix flour, sugar, lemon rind and salt. Add cut up butter and process until crumbed. Sprinkle with water and process to form a ball. Remove and flatten into a disc. Wrap in plastic wrap and refrigerate for 1 hour.

Preheat oven to 200°C (400°F)

Roll dough out on a lightly floured surface into a round. Place in sprayed 24cm (9 inch) tart tin. Freeze for 15 mins.

Cover the dough with foil and fill with either beans or rice. Bake for 10 minutes, then remove foil and beans and bake for a further 10-15 minutes until base is baked and lightly browned. Cool.

FILLING
4 EGGS
125ml (1/2 cup) SUGAR
80ml (1/3 cup) THICK CREAM
80ml (1/3 cup) FRESH LEMON JUICE
15ml (1 Tbs) LEMON RIND
PINCH SALT

Whisk all ingredients together. Pour filling into crust. Bake 25 mins. or until set. Cool completely.

Just before serving, preheat grill. Sprinkle 15ml (1 Tbs) sugar over tart and place under grill until sugar caramelises and browns. Serve warm or at room temperature.

SERVES 8

CHOCOLATE LOG WITH CHOCOLATE CREAM FILLING

CHUNKY CHOCOLATE CHIPPERS

Your family will love these chunky chocolate chip biscuits filled with nuts and cherries.

500ml (2 cups) FLOUR
5ml (1 tsp) BAKING POWDER
5ml (1 tsp) CINNAMON
5ml (1 tsp) SALT
185g (6 oz) UNSALTED BUTTER, SOFTENED
125ml (1/2 cup) SUGAR
125ml (1/2 cup) TREACLE BROWN SUGAR
2 EGGS
5ml (1 tsp) VANILLA ESSENCE
100g (3 1/2 oz) DARK CHOCOLATE CHIPS
250ml (1 cup) WHOLE GLACÉ RED CHERRIES
125ml (1/2 cup) PECANS, BROKEN INTO PIECES

Preheat oven to 180°C (375°F).

Line a baking tray with baking paper or an exopat mat.

Whisk flour, baking powder, cinnamon and salt in a small bowl. Beat the butter and both sugars well in a mixmaster until smooth and creamy. Add the eggs one at a time, until well blended and then add vanilla. Stir in the flour mixture on a low speed until just mixed.

Stir in chocolate chips, cherries and pecans with a spatula or wooden spoon. Drop spoonfuls of mixture onto the baking tray. Do not place them too close together.

Bake for 12-15 minutes or until golden underneath. Cool completely before placing in a Tupperware.

NOTE: These freeze beautifully. Defrost before using.

MAKES ± 24

PECAN SQUARES

Deliciously sticky, sweet and irresistible!

PASTRY
250g (8 oz) UNSALTED BUTTER
1ml (1/4 tsp) SALT
125ml (1/2 cup) CASTOR SUGAR
750ml (3 cups) FLOUR
1 EGG

Preheat oven to 180°C (375°F).
Line a large baking tray with foil extending over sides. Spray well with non-stick cooking spray.

In mixmaster, beat butter until soft. Add sugar and beat well to mix. Beat in egg and salt. Gradually add flour and continue mixing to form a dough. Press dough thinly into baking tray. Prick all over with a fork. Bake 20 mins.

PECAN TOPPING
250g (8 oz) UNSALTED BUTTER
125ml (1/2 cup) HONEY
60ml (1/4 cup) WHITE SUGAR
280ml (1 cup + 2 Tbs) TREACLE BROWN SUGAR
125ml (1/4 cup) CREAM
300g (9 oz) PECAN NUTS, CHOPPED COARSELY

TOPPING
Melt butter and honey in a small pot. Add sugars, stir to dissolve and boil without stirring for 2 mins. Remove from heat. Stir in cream and then nuts. Wait 5 mins. Spread sauce over biscuit base and bake for further 25 mins. Cool in baking tray for about 15 minutes. Cut with very sharp knife into squares and then allow biscuits to cool completely.

MAKES ± 48

SESAME CRISPS

An easy, crispy, crunchy biscuit, which will disappear as soon as you make them.

100g (3 1/2 oz) SHELLED GREEN PISTACHIOS
125ml (1/2 cup) WHITE SESAME SEEDS
175ml (3/4 cup) SUGAR
80ml (1/3 cup) FLOUR
90g (3 oz) UNSALTED BUTTER
80ml (1/3 cup) ORANGE JUICE

Preheat oven to 160°C (350°F).

Line a large baking tray with baking paper.

Process nuts, sesame seeds and sugar in food processor until nuts are crushed. Add flour and process to mix. Set aside. In the same bowl, process butter until softened and add orange juice and then return dry ingredients to the processor. Process again to mix.

Drop spoonfuls onto baking paper, spreading them thinly into circles. Bake for 10-15 minutes or until golden. Place on a baking rack to cool and crisp them.

NOTE: These can be made and kept in a Tupperware until ready to use.

MAKES ± 24

CHUNKY CHOCOLATE CHIPPERS,
PECAN SQUARES AND SESAME CRISPS

HOMEMADE SUN-DRIED TOMATO SAUCE

125ml (1/2 cup) SUN-DRIED TOMATOES, SOFTENED
125ml (1/2 cup) WATER
10ml (2 tsps) MUSTARD POWDER
5ml (1 tsp) GARLIC SALT
10ml (2 tsps) BASIL
45ml (3 Tbs) TOMATO PURÉE
80ml (1/3 cup) CIDER VINEGAR
1/4 ONION, CUT INTO PIECES
5ml (1 tsp) SALT
15ml (1 Tbs) HONEY

Process in food processor until as smooth as possible. Use as a replacement for the Ina Paarman Coat and Cook Sun-dried Tomato Sauce. Can be refrigerated for 10 days or frozen until ready to use.

TOMATO CHILLI JAM

400g (14 oz) ROSA CHERRY TOMATOES
30ml (2 Tbs) GINGER
2 RED CHILLIES
5ml (1 tsp) MINCED GARLIC
250ml (1 cup) SUGAR
125ml (1/2 cup) RED WINE VINEGAR
10ml (2 tsps) SALT

Place cherry tomatoes, ginger, chillies, and garlic in food processor. Process until finely chopped. Place mixture in a heavy pot and add sugar, red wine vinegar and salt. Boil uncovered for at least 30-40 minutes until thickened. (Mixture should still be a little runny, as it thickens when it cools.)

RED CURRY PASTE

10 RED CHILLIES, SOME SEEDED, ALL CHOPPED
15ml (1 Tbs) TOMATO PASTE
15ml (1 Tbs) LEMON JUICE
160ml (2/3 cup) OLIVE OIL
30ml (2 Tbs) FRESH CORIANDER
or PARSLEY, CHOPPED
5ml (1 tsp) FRESH GARLIC
5ml (1 tsp) FRESH GINGER
SALT
2 STICKS LEMONGRASS, CUT INTO PIECES, OUTER STALKS REMOVED

Process all ingredients in food processor until very finely chopped, or chop with mortar and pestle. Bottle and keep refrigerated until ready to use.

FLOUR TORTILLAS

500ml (2 cups) FLOUR
60ml ($^1/_4$ cup) PAREV (SHORTENING)
5ml (1 tsp) SALT
160ml ($^2/_3$ cup) WARM WATER

In a food processor, process parev (or shortening) and flour until it resembles fine breadcrumbs. Add salt to the water and pour into processor with the motor running until mixture forms a dough.

Allow to stand for 30 minutes in refrigerator covered in plastic wrap. Remove and divide into 12 balls. Then roll each one out into thin rounds.

Heat a frying pan. Spray with non-stick cooking spray and brown quickly on each side until golden. Place on a plate covered with foil until ready to use.

Reheat covered in microwave on high for 2-3 minutes just before serving.

SESAME OIL

30ml (2 Tbs) WHITE SESAME SEEDS, TOASTED
60ml ($^1/_4$ cup) OLIVE OIL

Heat sesame seeds dry in a frying pan. Add oil and heat gently. Cool and place in food processor and process or grind in mortar and pestle. Bottle until ready to use.

SWEET CHILLI SAUCE

125ml ($^1/_2$ cup) SUGAR
60ml ($^1/_4$ cup) WATER
80ml ($^1/_3$ cup) CIDER VINEGAR
5ml (1 tsp) SALT
15ml (1 Tbs) TOMATO SAUCE
1 RED CHILLI, CHOPPED
30ml (2 Tbs) CORIANDER, FINELY CHOPPED
30ml (2 Tbs) SPRING ONION, FINELY CHOPPED

Bring sugar, water, cider vinegar, salt and tomato sauce to a boil. Lower heat and simmer for about 5-8 minutes or until syrupy. Cool. Add coriander and spring onion and serve as a dipping sauce.

SWEET SOYA SAUCE

60ml ($^1/_4$ cup) SOYA SAUCE
30ml (2 Tbs) MOLASSES
30ml (2 Tbs) TREACLE BROWN SUGAR

Whisk all ingredients together. Heat on low to dissolve sugar. Keep bottled until ready to use.

TERIYAKI SAUCE

125ml ($^1/_2$ cup) SOYA SAUCE
10ml (2 tsps) GARLIC SALT
10ml (2 tsps) SUGAR
60ml ($^1/_4$ cup) WATER

Whisk all ingredients together.

WHITE OR RED WINE VINEGAR

250ml (1 cup) WHITE OR RED WINE
125ml ($^1/_2$ cup) WHITE VINEGAR
125ml ($^1/_2$ cup) WATER

Heat on stove until simmering. Cool and then keep in a bottle until ready to use.

Makes 2 cups.

WHOLEGRAIN MUSTARD

100ml ($^2/_3$ cup) YELLOW MUSTARD SEEDS
125ml ($^1/_2$ cup) WHITE WINE VINEGAR
80 ml ($^1/_3$ cup) OLIVE OIL
30ml (2 Tbs) HONEY
45ml (3 Tbs) TREACLE BROWN SUGAR
$^1/_4$ tsp TARTARIC ACID
60ml ($^1/_4$ cup) WATER
SALT TO TASTE

Soak mustard seeds in white wine vinegar overnight. Place them in food processor with remaining ingredients. Process. Adjust seasoning. Bottle and keep in a dark place for at least 2 weeks before using to allow flavours to mellow. Once opened, keep refrigerated.

Makes 1 cup.

Menu Ideas

THAI DINNER

Spicy Noodle Soup, 33
Seared Beef Salad, 45 or
Mixed Asian Salad, 41
Roasted Baby Vegetables with
Lemongrass Oil, 137
Asian Style Lamb, 95 or
Thai Fish Curry, 65
Grilled Figs, 147
Fig Ice Cream, 161

SUNDAY CASUAL

Phyllo Spirals, 7
Grilled Salmon Burgers, 63
Grilled Fish with Horseradish Sauce, 73
Fusilli with Asparagus Cream Sauce, 83
Shaved Feta Salad, 51
Caramelised Pears, 143
Grilled Bananas with Orange Salsa, 143
Baklava Ice Cream Loaf, 159

LADIES LIGHT LUNCH

Roasted Asparagus with Mustard
Mayonnaise, 5
Curried Pineapple Salad , 39
Festive Salad, 51
Tagliatelle Ai Funghi, 80
Seared Salmon on Tartare Mash, 69 or
Roasted Fish Steaks with Vegetables, 61
Steamed Chocolate Pudding, 145
Caramelised Lemon Tart, 179

WINTER WARMERS

Ginger Carrot Soup, 27
Pumpkin Bread, 13
Coq au Vin, 121
Ossobuco, 87 or
Lamb Shank Tagine with Couscous, 95
or Pollo Alla Toscana, 113
Steamed Chocolate Pudding, 145
Floating Island, 155 or
Fat Free Apple Pie, 167

SUNDAY BBQ

Meze Platter, 17 or
Baby Potato and Smoked Salmon
Salad, 15
Spiral Bread, 17
Grilled Chicken Kebabs, 111
Rack of Lamb with Mint Syrup, 105 or
Asian Style Lamb, 95 or
BBQ Beef Kebabs, 99
Roasted Potato Wedges, 137
Grilled Mushroom Kebabs, 127
Strawberry and Almond Salad, 43
Marinated Cabbage Salad, 39
Island Salad, 47
Fresh Fruit in Reduced Juice, 147
Pistachio Ice Cream, 157
Fruit Kebab Fondue, 143
Chocolate Meringues, 167

MEDITERRANEAN DINNER

Meze Platter, 17
Zucchini Muffins, 15
French Vegetable Soup, 29
Greek Lamb, 105 or
Lamb Shank Tagine with Couscous, 95
and
Coq au Vin, 121
Layered Roasted Vegetable Salad, 47
Grilled Figs and Nectarines, 147
Crème Caramel, 151
Chocolate Log with Chocolate Cream, 179

ITALIAN

Bruschetta al Pomodoro, 5
Tagliatelle ai Funghi, 80
Potato Gnocchi with Roasted Cherry
Tomatoes And Sage , 81
Tomato and Mozzarella Stacks with
Basil Cream, 11
Green Salad
Eggplant Rollatini, 133
Farfalle with Spinach, 85
Berry Tiramisu Filled Pavlova, 149
Chocolate Biscotti, 171
Grilled Fresh Fruit with Ginger
Mascarpone Sauce, 145

MEXICAN LUNCH

Mexican Cheese Pizza, 11
Mexican Steak Fajitas, 93
Mexican Tortilla Salad
(with or without cheese), 43
Fruit Kebab Fondue, 143
Fruity Ice Cream Parfait, 153
Mango Sorbet, 161

PASTA AND SALADS

Penne with Tomato-Herb Sauce, 80
Fusilli with Asparagus Cream Sauce, 83
or
Rigatoni with Zucchini Sauce and
Gremolata, 87
Roasted Butternut and Rosemary
Lasagne, 85 or
Low Fat Spinach and Vegetable
Lasagne, 87
Grilled Bananas with Orange Salsa, 143
or
Berry Tiramisu filled Pavlova, 149
Plum Tart and Plum Sorbet, 153/161
Florentine Tart, 175

LADIES LUNCH

Chilled Beetroot Soup, 33 or
Roasted Tomato Tarts, 9 or
Asparagus Vichysoisse, 31
Asparagus Phyllo Crisps, 13
Island Salad, 47 or
Layered Roasted Vegetable Salad
with Tahina Dressing, 47
Whole Stuffed Fish with Honey-Lime
Sauce, 71
Couscous Crusted Fish with Avocado
Salsa, 65
Roasted Baby Vegetables with
Lemongrass Oil, 137
Fresh Fruit in Reduced Juice, 147
Floating Island, 155
White Chocolate Cheesecake, 171

SUNDAY CELEBRATION TEA PARTY

Mixed Berry Nut Muffins, 169
Pecan and Jam Muffins, 175
Flourless Orange Cake, 177
Apple Phyllo Triangles, 173
Pistachio Crisps, 167
Cheeseless Grilled Vegetable Pizza, 7
Asparagus Phyllo Crisps, 13
Roasted Tomato Tarts, 9
Roasted Red Pepper and Eggplant Dip, 5

BAGEL AND COFFEE EVENING

Smoked Fish Terrine, 11
Marinated Sweet & Sour Salmon with Horseradish Sauce, 15 or
Baby Potato and Smoked Salmon Salad, 15
Zucchini Muffins or Spiral Bread, 15/17
Festive Salad, 51
Grilled Haloumi Salad with Tzatziki, 49
Blueberry Danish, 169
Assorted Biscuits, 181

FRIDAY NIGHT MEAT DINNER

Roasted Red Pepper and Tomato Soup, 25
Smoked Salmon Rosti with Wasabi Mayonnaise, 9
Lemon and Rosemary Chicken with Potatoes, 113 or
Sweet Chilli Chinese Chicken, 115
Sweet and Sticky Beef Ribs, 87 or
Herb-Crusted Prime Rib Roast, 103 or
Brisket with Caramelised Onions, 103
Mixed Squash Gnocchi with Sage Oil, 81
Stir-Fried Rice, 135
Tropical Asian Curry Vegetables, 135
Fruity Ice Cream Parfait, 153
Grilled Fresh Fruit with Ginger Mascarpone, 145
Floating Island, 155

FISH DINNER FOR 20

Caramelised Pear and Almond Salad, 49 or
Strawberry and Almond Salad, 43 or
Grilled Haloumi Salad, 49
Whole Stuffed Fish with Honey-Lime Sauce, 71
Baked Fish Strudels with Tomato Sauce, 67
Poached Linefish with Potatoes, Spinach and tarragon, 71
Potato Gnocchi with Roasted Cherry Tomatoes and Sage, 81
Pumpkin Pie, 127 or
Baked Assorted Pumpkin Wedges, 127
Glazed Roasted Baby Onions, 137
Shaved Mango Tart, 155 or
Apple Jalousie, 173
Banana Tarte Tatin, 151
Baklava Ice Cream, 159

LOWFAT DINNER

Eggplant Soup, 23
Toasted Barley, Chickpea and Carrot Salad, 53
Sweet and Spicy Breasts, 111 or
Veal Stir-Fry with Noodles, 99
Stir-fry Sliced Vegetables, 63
Jasmine Rice
Fresh Fruit in Reduced Juice, 147
Watermelon Granita, 159

LOW CHOLESTEROL

Marinated Sweet and Sour Salmon with Horseradish Sauce, 15
Lowfat Spinach and Vegetable Lasagne, 87
Honey-Mustard Glazed Fish, 59 or
Fish Fillets with Red Pepper Puree, 67 or
Crumbed Chicken Breasts with Cucumber Salsa, 111
Basmati Rice Pilaf, 128
Steamed Vegetables with Sesame Seeds, 131
Fresh Fruit in Reduced Juice, 147
Mango Sorbet, 161

DESSERT AND COFFEE

Apple Jalousie, 173
Chocolate Log with Chocolate Cream Filling, 179
Assorted Biscuits, 181
Banana Tarte Tatin, 151
Lemon, Lime and Lemongrass Ice Cream, 157
Grilled Fresh Fruit with Ginger Mascarpone, 145

BRUNCH

Roasted Red Pepper and Eggplant Dip, 5
Cheeseless Grilled Vegetable Pizza, 7
Smoked Salmon Rosti with Wasabi Mayonnaise, 9
Smoked Fish Terrine, 11
Marinated Sweet & Sour Salmon with Horseradish Sauce, 15
Pumpkin Bread, 13
Zucchini Muffins, 15
Baby Spinach, Tomato and Strawberry Salad, 41
Roasted Vegetable Tart with Sweet Onion Marmalade, 129
Apple Phyllo Triangles, 173
Banana Split Strudel, 149
Blueberry Danish, 169

Substitutes and Conversion

OVEN TEMPERATURES

°C	100	120	140	160	180	200	220	240	260	280
°F	200	250	300	350	375	400	425	450	475	500

MEASUREMENTS USED IN THIS BOOK

METRIC	IMPERIAL
2.5ml	1/2 tsp
5ml	1 tsp
7.5ml	1 1/2 tsp
10ml	2 tsps
15ml	1 Tbs

LIQUID CAPACITY

METRIC	IMPERIAL
60ml	1/4 cup
80ml	1/3 cup
125ml	1/2 cup
160ml	2/3 cup
175ml	3/4 cup
250ml	1 cup
375ml	1 1/2 cups
500ml	2 cups
750ml	3 cups
1 litre	4 cups
1.5litres	6 cups
2 litres	8 cups

WEIGHTS

30g	1 oz
60g	2 oz
90g	3 oz
125g	4 oz
155g	5 oz
180g	6 oz
200g	7 oz
250g	8 oz
300g	9 oz
310g	10 oz
375g	12 oz
500g	1lb or 16 oz
750g	1 1/2 lbs
1kg	2 lbs

TIN MEASUREMENTS

Smallest biscuit tray (baking sheet)	34 x 24 x 0.6 cm	13.5 x 9.5 x 20 inches
Large biscuit tray (baking sheet)	44 x 29 x 2.5 cm	17 x 11 x 1 inches
Small biscuit tray (baking sheet)	37 x 25 x 1 cm	14.5 x 10 x 40 inches
Loaf tins small	20 x 8.5 x 7cm	8 x 3.5 x 2.75 inches
medium	26 x 8.5 x 7cm	10 x 3.5 x 2.75 inches
large	35 x 11 x 7.5cm	14 x 4 x 3 inches
Pizza baking tin	31cm in diameter	12 inches
Spring form tins	24cm	9 inches
	26cm	10 inches
Tart tin small	26cm diameter	10 inches
large	28cm diameter	11 inches
Small roasting pan	330 x 230 x 50cm	13 x 9 x 2 inches
Large roasting pan	370 x 270 x 50cm	15 x 12 x 2 inches
Lamington (rectangular)	285 x 220 x 40cm	11 x 9 x 1.6 inches
Quiche large	28cm	11 inches

ALTITUDE CHANGES

The recipes in this book were tested at high altitude. This guide will help you alter your recipes accordingly if you are baking at sea level.

Baking powder - Increase by 0-0.5ml (1/4 tsp) for each 5ml (1 tsp) required.
Sugar - Increase by 15-30ml (1-2 Tbs) for each 250ml (1 cup) required.
Liquid - Decrease 15-30ml (1-2 Tbs) liquid per 250ml (1 cup) required.
Flour - Decrease by 15ml (1 Tbs) per 250ml (1 cup) required.
Baking temperature - Lower temperature by 10°C (25°F) and bake slightly longer

Appendix

Appendix

Appendix

BAKING PAPER

Available in all supermarkets, and is specifically for biscuits, cakes etc. as a non-stick lining placed on baking trays before baking. I find that it still requires spraying with non-stick cooking spray.

BOK CHOY

Chinese cabbage. Use in stir-frying instead of cabbage as it contains less water and does not give the food a cabbage taste. Available in most supermarkets.

COARSE NATURAL SALT

I prefer using natural sea salt crystals in all my cooking as it adds a special taste to the food. Salt grinders are available in all supermarkets. These use salt rocks, not crystals, which is why they need to be ground, as they do not dissolve easily. Crystals, however, dissolve easily, can be sprinkled on the food just before cooking, and bring out the best flavour.

COCONUT MILK

I like using Coconut Milk as opposed to the Cream, which is thicker, but either of them will be fine for the recipes. Please note that Coconut Milk does not contain dairy products.

EXOPAT (SILPAT) MAT

This is a specialised non-stick cooking mat made from silicone. It can withstand very high oven temperatures and can be used many times. It is washed with dishwashing fluid or a mild detergent, but can be used for both baking and cooking. The advantages are that the food browns very well, remains crispy, is non-stick and it can be lifted and used to slide the food off onto platters because it is very strong. Available from my cookery school and at speciality cookery stores.

FISH

South African linefish such as Kabeljou and Cape Salmon are firm, fleshy fish which are not too fishy. I prefer using these instead of Yellowtail or Tuna, because they tend to be very dry if overcooked. Equivalents in the United States would be Sea Bass, Halibut, Cod or Red Snapper, while Australian equivalents would be Blue-eyed Cod, Ling or Snapper.

Fish should always be measured at the thickest part of the fish to judge the cooking time. Use 10 minutes per 1 cm (0.4 inches) as your guide and you will always have perfectly cooked fish.

FLOUR

I only use cake flour, unless otherwise specified.

GARLIC

I find it easier to use ready-minced garlic. However, if you prefer crush your own cloves for a fresher taste. 1 crushed clove = $^1/_2$ tsp. minced garlic.

GRILLING OF PEPPERS

Preheat grill in oven. Place whole peppers on a baking tray and place directly under the grill until skin is charred on all sides. Then place them in a plastic packet for a few minutes to soften the skin for 10 minutes. Remove from packet, cut in half and run under a tap of cold water to remove skins and seeds.

HERBAMARE

This is a natural seasoning available from health shops worldwide (originally Swiss), which adds a wonderful flavour to all foods, particularly vegetables, chicken and fish. It does not contain MSG.

MASCARPONE SUBSTITUTE

See Sauces.

MEAT

South African meat is world renowned.

Steak cuts: Rump, Sirloin, T-bone and Porterhouse.
Roasts: Fillet, Sirloin, Rump and Topside.
Kosher Steak cuts: Side Bolo, London Broil, Blade Steak.
Kosher Roasts: Scotch Fillet, Bolo Roast, Chuck Roast, Top Rib Roast.

U.S. Steak cuts: NY Steak, Rib-eye or Top Sirloin.
U.S. Roasts: Trip-tip Roast, Sirloin Roast, London Broil.
U.S. Kosher steak cuts: Beef Rib Steak, Minute Steak, London Broil.
U.S. Kosher Roasts: Rib-Eye Roast, French Roast, Beef Chuck Roast.

MEAT MARINADE/ HOISIN SAUCE

An excellent kosher meat marinade is Meat Mate Classic which I use in place of Hoisin sauce. While not as thick and sweet, when diluted in a sauce it will suffice.

MAYONNAISE

I have generally specified a particular make of mayonnaise throughout the book, however, the use of "light mayonnaises" has become more popular since they are lower in calories. Kraft and Hellmann's Light are the most readily available. These are creamy mayonnaises and do not contain a lot of water, so they coat the food much better.

MOLASSES

Available in all supermarkets - Pouyoukas and Vital (South Africa).

NON-DAIRY CREAMER

I like to use Rich's Whip Kream Non-dairy Creamer for most of my ice creams, because it gives them a wonderful rich taste. However, it is not readily available (except from Nussbaum's in Johannesburg). Rich's also make a Whip Kream (Base), which can be diluted 2 to 1 and used as non-dairy milk in white sauces, custards etc. Other substitutes are Orly Whip or Instawhip (S.A). Haddar and Rich's can be found in Australia and the USA. It is important to remember that these all have a high palm oil content, so are extremely high in calories. Soya milk, however, while being non-dairy, cannot be whipped and adds a different taste to the food.

NON-STICK COOKING SPRAY

I like spraying casserole dishes, baking tins and roasting pans before using them as it makes cleaning much easier. If you oppose using spray, then greasing of tins and dishes can be done with butter or margarine.

OLIVE OIL

It is important to use a good quality olive oil and most Italian, cold pressed oils are excellent. A fruity olive oil will always give more flavour to the food. Be sure not to use an Extra Virgin Oil in salads, as these tend to be strong and can overpower the dressings. I cook mostly with a good quality olive oil, unless otherwise specified.

OLIVE OIL COOKING SPRAY

I use the natural Olive Oil Spray, although there are many different spiced varieties available. Spraying as a method uses far less oil.

PASSATA

A strained tomato puree from Italy sold in bottles of 700-750ml in most supermarkets worldwide. If unavailable, process 3 cans whole peeled Italian tomatoes and then strain to remove seeds and skin. Balance should be equivalent to 700-750ml.

PEPPER GRINDERS

I like using freshly ground black pepper for most foods. I find the bottled pepper much stronger with an artificial taste. However, if you prefer using white pepper, use it sparingly as it is much stronger than the freshly ground black variety.

POTATOES

Many different varieties are available. Baking potatoes are white and fluffy and are used for baking, gnocchi and mash potato. Waxy, yellow potatoes (Mediterranean) are used for casseroles.

PUFF PASTRY

It is important to use the best quality puff pastry available for best rising. I find that the pastry rises better if it is cold, as there will be minimum shrinkage.

RED HORSERADISH

A bottled horseradish available in the delicatessen or kosher section of most supermarkets.

ROMA TOMATOES

These are large Italian tomatoes called "Plum" tomatoes in some countries.

ROSA CHERRY TOMATOES

Small oval cherry tomatoes, which are much sweeter than the round variety. They are called "grape" cherry tomatoes, or baby Italian tomatoes in some countries.

STOCK CUBES

I have specified certain stock cubes or powders throughout the book because some give more flavour than others. The normal dilution of powder is 2 tsps to 1 cup of boiling water. Always dilute with boiling water in the amount specified according to the recipe. I have specified particular quantities in each recipe because I feel that dish requires additional flavouring. Herbamare can be diluted with water to make stock but will not give you a true stock flavour. Should you not wish to use products which contain MSG, there is a range of liquid stocks available throughout most supermarkets locally, which do not contain MSG and are completely natural. These only require the addition of salt.

SUN-DRIED TOMATO SAUCE

For substitute see Sauces. I usually use Ina Paarman Coat & Cook Sun-dried Tomato Sauce.

SUN-DRIED TOMATOES IN VINAIGRETTE

I use the Ina Paarman sachets, but any soft sun-dried tomatoes mixed with an Italian vinaigrette will do the trick.

SUN-DRIED TOMATO PESTO
I use the Ina Paarman sachet. If unavailable, process some softened sun-dried tomatoes in a food processor with a little olive oil to make your own.

SWEET CHILLI SAUCE
See Sauces for home-made or purchased bottled Sweet Chilli Sauce in most supermarkets.

SWEET MAYONNAISE
These generally are the local variety and range from Nola to Crosse and Blackwell.

SWEET POTATO
Also called "yams" in other countries.

TAH TSAI
Chinese Spinach - remains crispy when stir-fried.

TAHINA
A sesame seed sauce made with garlic, parsley, olive oil, water and seasonings. Available ready-made in most delicatessens or from Middle Eastern supermarkets.

TERIYAKI SAUCE
See Sauces. Can be home-made or purchased.

TOMATO SALSA
I use a "mild" or "medium" salsa under the brand name "Old El Paso". MasterFoods Chunky Salsa is also available in South Africa.

TORTILLAS
These are flour tortillas, sold as "Burrito" Tortillas in South Africa under the "Old El Paso" brand name.
See recipe in Sauces for home-made tortillas.

TREACLE BROWN SUGAR
This is a sticky brown sugar, called "Treacle" in South Africa. It is called "Soft Brown Sugar" in other countries.

WASABI POWDER
Available in most Chinese supermarkets in powder form. Dilute with water to make a paste.

WHOLEGRAIN MUSTARD
This contains mustard seeds which add texture to the mustard. Available in most supermarkets. The MasterFoods Wholegrain mustard is available in South Africa and is considered kosher under the NSW Beth Din, Australia. If unavailable, see recipe in Sauces section.

YEAST
I enjoy the availability and ease of "Instant Yeast". Always check the label to ensure that you have the "instant" yeast, as "Active and Brewers" do not work identically. This dry variety does not need to be "proofed" like a fresh cake of yeast. A packet of Instant Yeast weighs 10g or measures 1 heaped Tbs. A cake of fresh yeast is 25g = 1 packet Instant Yeast.

Index

Index

Index

A

B

C

E

F

G

S

T

V

W

Z